KWA MABINTI

KWA MABINTI

Australia: The Land of My Healing

PURITY

Library of Congress Control Number:		2017900131
ISBN:	Hardcover	978-1-5245-2137-0
	Softcover	978-1-5245-2136-3
	eBook	978-1-5245-2135-6

Print information available on the last page.

Rev. date: 01/04/2017

To order additional copies of this book, contact:
Xlibris
1-800-455-039
www.Xlibris.com.au
Orders@Xlibris.com.au
746002

K wa Mabinti, is a Swahili phrase meaning 'to daughters'. This is to all the daughters (all women are daughters to someone) out in the world who have had similar experiences or worse. There is hope, and if God healed me, he can heal you too.

To my daughters, Light and Beauty, I pray that God will use my story to encourage you and to remind you of his mercies and goodness all the days of your life. May it teach you how to forgive others as God forgives you, and remind you that none of us are righteous and good; therefore, all of us need God's forgiveness.

And to my dear little sister whose name means 'Pearl', you are precious. I watch as you live a life so similar to my own. I pray that you will find comfort and strength herein and know that you are never alone. God is never too far from us, and neither is he deaf to our cries even though sometimes it feels like he is. Though I am so far away, know that I am here for you and I love you even with your imperfections, mistakes, emotions, and all.

Life is always about perspective, and godly perspective is the best. I hope you will seek God's perspective in every experience you have in this life. God bless you all as you grow up to be God's servants.

CHAPTER ONE

Kwa Mabinti

One morning, in mid-April of 2016 at about 3 a.m., with tears in my eyes and sadness in my heart I reflected on my life. I felt lost, misunderstood, alone, and forgotten. I felt sorry for myself, as if the world was against me.

My life is riddled with many moments like these—of feeling like a victim. Sometimes I am sad, will cry and ask, 'Why me?' And then I remember how far God has brought me and seen me through. Then I remember who I really am. Sometimes I do feel lost in this foreign land that has become my new home. It is as if my life before did not matter and did not happen.

It is because of this that I decided to write this book so that you, dear daughters, would know about that past, who I was, where I have been and why I am who I am. I looked up one day and realised that my life before 1 January 2011 had been swept under the carpet and forgotten. My experiences were just another part of life to others, but those experiences and the memories I have had shaped me into who I am today. To ignore them or to forget them will be to bury who I am, where I have been and the lessons I have learnt along the way.

The experiences we have in life, no matter how painful, are meant to be used to help and bless others. God created us for community and for fellowship with him and one another. It's no wonder he says 'to love your neighbour as yourself'. Going through a painful experience and not sharing with another in need helps no one. Someone else needs to know that they too can make it through, that there's hope. Reach out and help pull them out. By doing so you help yourself or allow yourself to heal.

CHAPTER TWO

There were once three men. Each was given a big, heavy package with their name on it to carry. The instruction was to carry the packages to their homes some distance away.

The first man picks up the package and bows under the weight. He starts sweating but is determined to carry it the whole way. He takes a step at a time, his mind focused on the destination. Each step becomes more laborious than the last but he knows in his heart that if he puts it down, even for a second, he will not be able to lift it up again. He meets a few people on the way and they ask him if they can help. He painfully shakes his head no and keeps moving along. After all, it is his package. It has his name on it. He continues until he collapses, and dies, metres from his house. He doesn't make it and he dies not knowing what it is he was carrying.

The second man, like the first, picks up the package and starts on his way. After only a few steps he sets the package on the ground and sits on it to rest. He knows it will take him a long time to get the package home but decides he will get it there one way or another. He sits there thinking about how heavy the package is, wondering what is in it, and regretting ever receiving it. Once in a while he gets up, picks it up, walks a few steps and puts it down again. His breathing heavy, his body sweating, he sits on the package again to catch his breath. Just as before, he sits there thinking of the burden that he is sitting on and feels sorry for himself. He looks up and sees the front door to his house—so near yet so far. He tries pushing the box without luck. He tries pulling, but to no avail. He has to carry it! He sits there for a long time and the more he sits, the more frustrated, angry, stressed, sad, panicked and anxious he gets.

Many pass him by and ask if they can help. He talks about the package, how heavy it is, and about how frustrated he is by it. He complains to anyone who cares to listen but accepts no help from anyone. After a really long time he finally makes it home. He is exhausted, angry, emaciated, and is an emotional mess. He slowly opens the package and can't believe what he sees. This is what he has been carrying around? If only he knew earlier. He dies in pain and regret of having carried around so much.

The third man lifts the package. He feels the weight of it and sets it down. He turns to the person who has given him the package and asks what it was. The man tells him that whatever is in it is his, but he has to carry it home. No one else can help him carry it or show him how to carry it. He has to work that out himself. The third man stands there and thinks. He gets an idea. He knows he can't carry the package; it would kill him before he gets home. He decides to open the package and see what is in it.

Inside he finds sticks, rocks and dirt. But among all that rubbish, he finds the smallest of jewels. They shine in the light in the brightest of colours. He works his way through the whole box, slowly throwing away the rubbish and getting the treasures. After a while he gets to the bottom of the box and has a handful of brilliantly coloured treasures. He puts them in his pocket, next to his heart, and walks home a happy man.

On the way he passes the second man, still complaining about the big package he was sitting on. He tries to help by suggesting he should probably open it and sort through the mess to get his treasure. The second man thinks this too simple a solution and ignores him. He decides complaining and whining about it is easier. He passes by the first man who is trying to ignore the large package on his back. He suggests he puts it down and goes through it, but like the second man he ignores him. He decides carrying it and ignoring it is easier. After all, it is none of his business and he does not understand. The third man walks on and gets home safe, sound, and happy with treasures close to his heart.

The man who gave the packages is life. The package is the bad experiences we have in this life. Life does dish us up some awful stuff sometimes and the three men represent how we deal with these issues and situations. Home represents the latter years of our life.

The first man is determined to do it all by himself. He always carries whatever burden it is by himself. He tries to forget it is there, so bitterness, anger, revenge, and stress grows in his heart. Eventually it kills him. He dies young, never reaching the age God had set for him. The second man acknowledges the experience happened. He too tries to carry it by himself. He knows it is something he has to face one way or another. Once in a while he puts it down but doesn't shut up about it. These are the people who are always talking about their experiences, looking for sympathy from anyone and everyone. But when asked to seek for help, they say it is not an issue anymore. They then pick it up again and strain under its weight. They never fully process it and deal with it. They never let God heal them. The people they meet along the way are God-sent people who have either dealt with the same issue and are healed, or people gifted by God to be able to help. Sometimes, it is even God himself who asks to help, but they let none help just like the first man. Consequently they are stuck in the same place for years, and possibly all their life. Eventually they die sad and regretful for having not put the burden down.

The third man is a rare species. These are the people who acknowledge the experience. They acknowledge that they have to carry it but are clever enough to give themselves time to deal with it. They open it up, deal with all the rubbish, seek help and let God in to heal them. The treasures are the little nuggets of gold they get from it. These are the positives from the bad experience (yes, even the worst experience has some good in it.) The Bible does say in Rom 8:28 that 'all things work for good for those who love God'. Note that it says all things, not only good things, and not some things, but *all*. Good can be found in the most painful experiences and sometimes one has to sift through the rocks, dirt and the rubbish to get the gems.

I have been the second man for the longest time. I acknowledged the bad that happened to me. I talked about it. Sometimes I would go for days, months, and even years without even thinking about it. Like the second man, I was sitting on it, trying to ignore it but acknowledging it every turn. Then I would get up, pick it all up again and get angry, frustrated, and pitiful all over again. I kept asking 'why me, why me?' As if it is God who did the terrible things to me.

I refuse to keep feeling like a victim and being a victim anymore. Now I have decided to put the 'package' down, open it up and sort through the mess. I'm letting God heal me and deal with each issue one at a time. I'm becoming like the third man in the story, and this book is part of that process. Yes, I am finding a lot of rubbish going through those painful memories at times but along with it comes the most amazing little treasures. How I praise God for those little gems. After all, I am the sum total of all my experiences. They helped shape me into who I am.

CHAPTER THREE

Daughters, my story is long and complicated, and I know I can't cover it all in one book. Every time I want to start telling it I'm lost as to where I should start and whether it is worth telling. There's also a rush of emotions—emotions I was not ready to deal with. So with so many false starts I have shelved it for years. I will be as honest and open as possible and I will try to remember as much as I can, but I do know that I cannot fit thirty years of experiences in one book. I also believe it is a story that needs to be told and one that I hope will help others in their own journey in this life.

One early morning on a cool morning in central Kenya, on 28 June 1987, at about 4 a.m., a baby girl named Purity was born. My mum was born 4 June 1951 to Ron and Esther. Mum was the sixth born in a family of eleven. She had four elder sisters, two younger sisters, one elder brother and three younger brothers. She was particularly close to her immediate elder sister, Grace, and shared a lot of her secrets with her. Unfortunately Aunt Grace passed away in 2015 with a lot of those secrets, and I was unable to go pay my last respect as I was in Australia. Mum respected her second eldest, Hannah, like she did her mum. My mother, Sarah, was a secretary at a school and my dad was a teacher at the same school. She loved singing and serving in church. She loved writing too.

The one thing that stood out the most about my mum was her individuality. Even as a little girl I realised she did things her own way, dressed in her own way and spoke her mind. She respected herself and respected others but she did not conform to what others did around her.

I remember her afro most of all. Sometimes I would be embarrassed by what looked like unkempt hair when I was growing up and I would hardly share photos of Mum with others because of that. Now that I am older and wiser, I am proud that she was confident enough to love her hair as it was and loved herself as she was.

Mum had the most beautiful smile, with a gap between her front upper teeth. I loved that gap and as a child I had one too. I loved being just like Mum. Sadly after losing my milk teeth the gap disappeared. The opposite happened with my brother, Ethan. I was truly sad and disappointed to have lost that one thing that I thought made me like Mum. In my childlike mind Mum was the greatest person I knew (as children often think of their mums).

I had a normal early childhood, but I remember dancing around a charcoal *jiko* in a baby blue dress when I was around three. I fell in head first. I then did almost the exact same thing when I was five or six. This time, however, I sat in it! I remember the second one better than the first, as I remember Mum taking me to school and having to lie on my tummy all day, as I could not sit. My whole behind was really burnt and I distinctively remember the scab. I would sit and try break a piece at a time to the horror of my parents.

Things changed when I was six. I remember that birthday as if it was yesterday. Mum surprised me at school with two or three big plastic bags of snacks to share with my friends. In my mind's eye I can see her with a bright smile. I can clearly see the gap in her top two teeth and the bags in her hands. She never forgot my birthday and always made a big deal of it. Unfortunately that was the second last birthday I'd celebrate in a long time.

My mum and I had a really good relationship. She was my friend, but my mum too when I needed her to be. She was a talented seamstress and she always made us matching outfits. We had a song every time we had the matching outfits on. The song went like this, *'Nguo fanano, nguo fanano. Ingine inanuka mafi ya kuku.'* It is loosely translated to *'Matching dress, matching dress, and one smells like chicken poo'*. We would point at each other's dress in turn for each syllable and the dress at the end of the song will be the chicken poo dress. Oh, how we laughed hard each time. It became my special thing with Mum.

I loved going to her bed every morning and sleeping in with her, or just talking and playing. I would fall asleep sometimes and she would sneak out and get ready for work. This is also one thing that my daughter loves doing. She is one who reminds me most of my mum.

Mum loved outings too. I remember we went to nature and tourist places many times in those early years, and took a lot of photos as evidence of the same. In fact, it seemed almost every weekend we were out somewhere, watching and listening to nature, watching the tourists going about their business of buying curios, taking photos, and just marvel at the beautiful creation around us.

I remember lying on the ground next to mum one day as she did laundry. I was looking up into the sky, singing and chatting. One particular day I had not realised I was lying on a hole (the hole was well-covered by the grass, and I had put my head on it). Next thing I know I feel movement around my head, and when I stood up to look, there was a frog! I was so scared and anxious, and that's when I started biting my nails. I can't remember any more details of the day, what Mum said or did, but that has stayed with me for a while.

Mum was also a disciplinarian. She never let my brothers and I get away with anything. We lived with two of my elder stepbrothers, and Mum and Dad had my younger brother, Ethan, who was two years younger than I am. The four of us got into so much mischief! Mum and Dad worked all day at the school. They would sometimes lock us in the house because they couldn't afford a housemaid or there was no one to look after us. On these days we got into so much trouble. We would literally trash the house playing house or whatever else our imaginations would create. I have a memory of Mum coming home one day and finding a trail of caked sugar, salt, and water from the kitchen to the bedroom. We had poured water, salt, and sugar all over the floor and in the beds, and it had dried up and solidified. She wasn't happy. Mum did not smack, she pinched, and she had lovely long nails. I can still feel that pinch from memory. My stepbrother, Dan, still remembers those pinches too.

CHAPTER FOUR

One Saturday afternoon, in the second half of 1993, Mum came home from work. My younger brother, Ethan, and I were playing. I have no idea where my stepbrothers were at that time, but they were not living with us. She called me and asked if I could get her a mattress, as she was feeling unwell. She said she had a headache and wanted to lie outside in the sun. I brought out a little foam mattress. Ethan and I were really hungry, as we had not had lunch, so I went to Mum and told her so. We had been waiting for her to make us some lunch, so we had been excited to see her, only for her to go lie outside unwell. She asked me to be a big girl and go cook something for my brother and me.

I was so honoured and felt so proud that Mum had trusted me with a job so big. I couldn't stop smiling as Ethan and I went into the house and I decided to make rice, as I had seen Mum make so many times. I put the stove on and put water in a saucepan. I don't even think I let it boil before I put the rice in. The two of us just stood there watching it and we impatiently took out the rice prematurely, served it into bowls, and went to sit next to Mum as we ate our partially cooked, mostly raw, rice. But I was so proud I had done something so grown-up. By this time Mum looked really sick; and even though she could see the rice was not really cooked, there was nothing she could do.

As we lived in a school compound, the news spread like wild fire that Mum had left work unwell. One neighbour came around to check on Mum, found her asleep and us eating rice. She felt sorry for us, went to her house and brought us some food. We were so hungry and we didn't see what the big deal was.

The next few weeks seemed to move really fast and in a blur. There were many visits to the doctors and many more second opinions. Nobody seemed to know what was wrong with Mum and the headache that randomly started one Saturday afternoon never left. One thing that most doctors agreed on was that Mum was becoming blind and needed glasses. Mum did not like that idea at all. She was becoming long-sighted, I think they said, but Mum kept going to different doctors, looking for a diagnosis instead of dealing with one symptom of whatever was causing the headaches.

One Wednesday in October (I think it was), I was awoken by some commotion very early in the morning. My bed was in the sitting room with a big curtain dividing it from the rest of the room. We lived in a two-bedroom house, so my parents had one room and my brothers the other. Anything that happened in the living room, I could hear, as I didn't have a door or wall to keep the sound away. Anyway, on this particular morning, Dad and Mum had breakfast, a shower and packed a bag. When they noticed I was awake Mum told me she was going to Nairobi to the bigger hospital so they could treat her. She asked me to go back to sleep and I would see her soon. I pretended to go back to sleep but as soon as I heard the door closed behind them I was up and looking out the window. I saw them walking toward the school gate about 300 metres away and on the other side of the gate was a white car waiting for them. I watched them until they got in and with one look toward the house, they were gone. That was the last I saw Mum. She never came back. I never saw her soon as she promised.

Dad began going to the hospital every day or every other day in the next few months, so he had to get maids to help us out and keep the household running. Every evening the school workers, who were Christians like Mum, would gather at our house and would pray, sing and ask Dad about Mum's health. This went on for about two months.

One day Dad took my brother, Ethan, and me with him to Nairobi. I was wearing a pair of brown leather shoes and they were hurting my feet. My parents used to say my feet grew like trees because I would outgrow a pair of shoes in two weeks. I loved shiny pumps but Mum would buy them and two weeks later I would be whinging in pain. So with Mum in hospital Dad had to buy me shoes, and he chose the most hardy, boyish, long-lasting shoes he could get—brown lace leather shoes! As I had used them to their two-week sell by date, I was once again whinging and carrying on about how they were pinching my toes. When we got to Nairobi Dad decided to leave me with his lady cousin who had a second hand clothes stall in a busy market area, as he and Ethan went on their way. I was happy to be off my feet for a while. Little did I know they had gone to see Mum.

When they got back, my 4-year-old brother Ethan was excited and he kept saying they had seen Mum. He also said she looked really sick. A couple of days later he looked at me sadly and said that the place where Mum was is really dirty and some people had to share a bed. I was saddened and angry at Dad and the dirty hospital. I couldn't understand why Dad had not told me we were going to see Mum and I couldn't understand why Mum had to suffer or why she had to be in that dirty place. 'We have to go back soon at some point,' I thought to myself. 'I would see mum too.'

On the eighteenth of December, as usual Dad went and the worshippers came to the house. Something was different on this day though. Dad was late coming back. Us kids had been sent to bed and from the safety of my bed I listened to them sing and pray through the curtain as they waited for Dad. He finally came home and when he walked in they welcomed him and asked of news of my mother. He was silent. Then, slowly, he began to speak. The room was dead silent apart from Dad's voice. I will never forget the words that came from his mouth.

A few days earlier the doctors had decided to do brain surgery on Mum. As usual I listened in as Dad explained all about it. From his description Mum's beautiful afro had been shaved off and her head cut ear to ear and forehead to back. The doctors were still trying to figure out what was causing the headache, as they still had no idea. In my 6-year-old head, I was trying to imagine what my mum would look like with no hair and stitches on her head. I remember Dad saying something about medicine being put in her head and again, in my imagination, I saw the doctors putting actual Panadol in Mum's brain! On this day, the eighteenth of December, after the surgery the doctors had declared they had no idea what was happening, but that they thought the surgery went fine.

'She passed away at about 2 a.m.,' Dad said. 'She had a cardiac arrest.' The silence! I heard the door open and one by one the worshippers left, each quietly saying sorry to Dad and sobbing. I was lost in my own world. What Dad said had not sunk in. I was lost in my own thoughts, so much so that I didn't hear the last person leave or Dad closing the door, putting the light out and going to bed. He was broken and sad that the woman he loved was gone. Like most African fathers he never showed his sadness, never mentioned Mum again, and life went on. Mum was gone but I didn't know how to process that. I really didn't understand it at all.

CHAPTER FIVE

The next few days were a blur. I remember standing with my brother at a distance, with my Aunt Hannah, as we watched a crowd of people looking into a box. She was holding our hands and at one point she went to look in the box, leaving us in the hands of another. I had on a beautiful sky blue dress, the same shade of dress I had on when I fell in the fire. I was also wearing socks and Dad's favourite brown leather shoes. Everyone seemed sad and in a sombre mood. My 4-year-old brother and I had no idea what was going on. Everybody we knew and didn't know was there. The workers who had faithfully gathered in our house every night for the two months were there, my uncle and aunties and my paternal grandma who had never come to Nairobi (and never did again apart for my wedding). My brother and I knew something big was happening but could not understand what it was.

We were ushered into a waiting vehicle and joined a convoy that ended up at my maternal grandparents' home. I was glad to be at Grandpa's and to see my cousins and other relatives. Once again I was amazed at the number of people gathered. I went about the business of catching up with cousins. I was really irritated when the adults kept directing us to different places, trying to keep us quiet and calm through whatever it is that was going on.

Shortly after, I was standing in my Uncle Steven's living room. The box, now closed and covered with a white table cloth, was in there. Close family members were in there with us and the room felt so crowded. I just wanted to get out! The box had really lovely flowers on it. I remember noticing the reds, the orange, the white, the yellow.

I had no idea what the adults were talking about, but someone prayed as I admired the mounds of beautiful flowers. Soon, we were out. This time my dad, brother, and I were given front row seats and we listened to one person after the other talking. They were all talking about Mum I figured because they kept mentioning her name. Nice things were being said about her. I knew we were at Grandfather Ron's because of Mum but I didn't want to understand that this was her funeral. After a long time we were in front of a hole in the ground and the big box was put in the hole.

I remember the songs we sang 'Rock of Ages', 'My Faith Looks up to thee', 'Nearer my God to thee', 'How Great Thou Art'. Now and then I hear another hymn being sang and it takes me back to that day. Every time I hear any of those songs tears flow freely. They've become Mum's goodbye songs to me and they have become associated with sadness, death and loss. We sang as we watched the box go down and then we were given soil to throw into the hole. Just like that, it was done and lunch was being served. I ran off to catch up with uncle, aunts, and cousins. I was not hungry, though, but was forced to eat something.

After having lunch my dad's relatives, who had come all the way from afar, Dad, my brother, and I got into vehicle and away we went. It was about 3 p.m. and we embarked on an eight-hour journey to Dad's ancestral home. The date was 24 December 1993, Christmas Eve. Nobody talked about Sarah again after that day, not in my presence anyway. All I know about her are the memories that the little 6-year-old had. Sometimes it feels like she had never been here in the first place.

We got to Dad's ancestral just before midnight. There were bonfires all over Grandma Hadassah's front yard. Again, there were so many people around and for the third time that day I wondered what all the fuss was for. What was the special occasion?

I ran off to sit with my cousins and particularly my elder cousin, Nora. She wasn't much older but I always saw her as more mature and she made me comfortable. I asked her why all these people were here and she, without pausing, said, 'Well, they are all here for your mum's funeral. We all thought you were bringing her body and have her buried here.'

I replied, 'No, we went to Mum's home.'

Again I found myself talking but in the back of my head I knew Mum was coming back. I didn't understand why people looked so sad and kept talking about Mum as if she had gone forever. I was still going to wait for her to come back home.

We didn't really sleep that night. We sat around the fires and chatted away. It was a very unique Christmas; it didn't feel like Christmas.

6 a.m. Christmas morning came and Nora and I were still sitting around chatting. From a distance I saw a woman I had never seen before coming toward Grandma Hadassah's house. There were still lots of people in the compound, friends and strangers to me, but this particular one caught my attention straight away. I turned to Nora and asked who she was. I'll never forget what she said, 'That's your step-mum, Elisa. She is the mother of your stepbrothers.' My spirit sank. I remember feeling panicked and fearful, and I ran the opposite direction away from Grandma's house. I don't remember much after that but that initial reaction to her has always stayed with me.

Christmas season has never been the same. It reminds me of Mum and the day we said goodbye to her. It has become a time for mourning, loss, and a celebration for me for years to come—a bittersweet time.

CHAPTER SIX

In the New Year Dad took us back to 'normal' life. We still had different housemaids but none lasted. These maids came from all manner of backgrounds and faiths. We children would go to whatever church they went to, so we went to Catholic, Baptist (it was my favourite as the children were given sweets for correct answers to questions asked), Presbyterian, Pentecostal, African Inland (this is the church Mum used to go and her dad was a pastor in this church).

But as I said the maids didn't last, as they always did something wrong, stole something or spread diseases. I got lice and scabies, I remember, and when Dad would tell them to leave or when they decided to leave we had to inspect their bags. Often there was something they were stealing from us. Dad really got tired of them.

He couldn't remarry yet, so he had four children to look after, worked full time and needed help, so he kept hiring help. In Dad's culture, one cannot remarry within twelve months of losing a spouse, otherwise it is believed he had something to do with the spouse's death. It is for the sake of the surviving spouse's total healing before jumping into another relationship.

I remember one night I burst out crying, as it finally dawned on me that Mum was not coming back. She was gone and I wasn't going to see her again. My heart broke into pieces that night and I was never the same again. I was seven years old, it was a year after Mum was buried.

Years later, when I visited my grandparents, I saw the most beautiful red hibiscus plant growing on Mum's grave. When I first saw it, my mind went back to the day in my uncle's house as I looked at the beautiful flowers on what I had come to acknowledge was Mum's casket. I smiled as I looked at the deep green leaves and the deep red flowers. Mum's hometown is not known for its agricultural favourable weather. The place is nearly a desert. People farmed not knowing whether anything would grow because it is a very dry place. But here, surrounded by dryness and unrelenting heat, was a healthy, brightly coloured bush full of the brightest red flowers. It spoke volumes. To me, it was God assuring me that mum was okay. Oh, what a great comfort that was.

At around the same time my stepbrothers started verbally abusing me and I noticed this would escalate every time they came back from their mum's place. They would tell me to go look for my father, that my dad was not my father, and they didn't want me there stealing their father from them. They used my brother, Ethan, to hit me with lots of things. Sticks, stones and a padlock were all used at some point because I was following them around. I just wanted to play and be with my brothers, step or not. I didn't understand why they hated me so much, what I had done to them, or anyone. I was sad and confused but tried not taking things to heart. I didn't believe the things they were telling me. If he was not my father, why did he answer to Dad, and why was I in his house?

By the end of 1994, Dad had just about given up on house girls. He instead brought a friend of his called John to look after us. John was in his late twenties or early thirties in my 7-year-old estimation. He was tall and always seemed like a giant to me. He was not big though, but slim and fit. He scared me from the beginning. But he was Dad's friend. He worked well, Dad and him seemed to get along well, so when Dad lost his job at the end of that year, he moved with us to our new home too.

Dad, losing his job in the school he had worked at with Mum, was another blow to my little self. The owner of the school had promised at the funeral to look after us because my mum had done a great job for her. Ironically, the only photo of Mum's funeral I have is of the school's principal, the owner of the school, giving a speech. But a few weeks shy to Mum's passing anniversary she fired Dad and didn't care what happened to him and us. It was years later, after university, that Dad reminded me of the promises she made at Mum's funeral and how none of it was ever kept. By that stage I had learned that people promise one thing but when the rubber met the road they were nowhere to be seen.

We once again had a two-bedroom house within the school compound where Dad worked. And again, my dad had one bedroom, while my brothers and John had the other. I was the wild card who would either sleep on the floor in Dad's room, the boy's room, or the sitting room. My life completely changed in that little house and the horror that became my life still feels like a nightmare.

CHAPTER SEVEN

John was a typical houseboy. He would finish his chores early, have nothing to do for the rest of the day and so would be out chasing after house girls in the compound and surrounding areas. He would come home and, when Dad was asleep, would share his adventures with my elder brother. I heard a lot because these were the times I was sleeping in their room. The days he had not convinced anyone to sleep with him he would be so frustrated and once again he would share that frustration. My conclusion from his story was that men could not survive without sex and were like animals. That disgusted me, even as a child. I kept wondering why he had no self-control at all and why men treated sex as oxygen.

One day he started buying me sweets whenever he was out grocery shopping. Of course sweets were not something we had lying around in the house and Dad didn't encourage eating it, so I knew enough to hide it from Dad and enjoyed each one of them.

Next thing I know John, after discussing his exploits or not with the neighbourhood maids, would start talking about me and how that night he would go to my bed. My brother, Dan (he is 3 years older so he was only 10) would be his audience. I never heard Liam talking so I assume he was asleep at this point.

And come to my bed he did. He would make me touch him, rub him. He would remove my panty and would lie on me, rubbing himself on me until he ejaculated. I think he did not dare go all the way because blood or pain would have been too great an evidence against him to Dad. Doing it this way it was going to be his word against mine. Then he would casually get up, thank me, get back into his bed, and tell Dan all about it as I curled up in a ball and silently cried. The next day he would bring me more sweets and threaten me not to tell anyone of what was happening. On the days I would resist, I would have a miserable day the next day. He would make me do more chores, beat me or generally treat me badly. I was terrified of him.

This became my life. I dreaded nightfall! I would be curled up in a corner, praying that today he wouldn't come, but then he would. I wet my bed to further embarrass myself. I would get up in the morning with my mattress and bedding to wash and hang outside. I was eight. I don't know whether the bed-wetting started with the abuse or was enhanced by it or whether I just had never stopped from childhood. Either way, instead of it getting better, it got worse. My brothers would laugh at me, my dad lecture me, and John would make me wash, hang and bring in my bedding.

I don't know whether Dad sensed something was going on because he suddenly asked that I start sleeping on the floor in his room, but after a few days he couldn't stand the smell of my bedding so I was exiled to the sitting room. The problem was my brothers' bedroom was off the sitting room while Dad's was down the hall, so John would come to my bed in the dead of night and none was the wiser. After a while I was sent back to the boys' room as no one could stand the smell in the sitting room and the cycle went on.

I was afraid to sleep, I hated being in the house, I hated darkness, I hated John with his satisfied smile. During the day, when no one was looking, he would poke his tongue in and out in a suggestive manner or wink in my direction. I didn't just hate him I loathed him! But at least he 'paid' for the things he was doing to me. I got sweets. I started to expect him and enjoy whatever he was doing. To me that was all I was for, that was to be my life, so I better enjoy it instead of being so miserable. I learned to accept things as they were and deal with them.

On the flip side, dawn was my friend. I loved sunshine. I got up really early in the morning, had breakfast, did my chores, and ran out to play. I was often the first one out and the last one in. I found myself praying over and over again for the day not to end, as I knew the nightmare that awaited me in the house. I had to be called in for lunch quite a few times because I preferred not to go in for lunch. But the end of the day did come and the nightmare did continue. My friends never knew what was happening behind closed doors. To them I was a happy little girl who loved life and church. I even had the hottest guys in the compound fighting over me and I could pick and choose who I wanted to be my boyfriend.

My first boyfriend was Caleb. He was about two years older. All the girls thought he was really cute and were really jealous he had eyes just for me. A guy called Peter shed tears when I rejected him for this hunk that had recently moved in. I was eight going on nine when we first met and we dated for a little over three years. That was the longest relationship I have ever had, save for the one I am in now with my husband. Our relationship was about letters and poetry. We wrote and wrote a lot of letters to each other over that period and when we were out with the other kids we would get on as if nothing was happening. Our mutual friend, Chloe, was our post-girl and she would pass the letters one to the other. We never held hands and never kissed. Ours was a romance of words. I liked it and loved him.

He had no idea what was happening in my family. The insults from my brothers, which had started to die down at this point, and the sexual assault, which was almost a daily occurrence. I never hinted it to any of my friends because I was embarrassed about it and didn't want to be judged as a whore. I felt like one and knew I was one. Even in my naïve young mind, I knew what was happening was wrong, but I thought I was the one doing the wrong. Well, I guess they will know now reading this.

One evening in August of 1996, Dad walked in with a woman. He had been single since Mum died and the stress of being a single parent was great. He needed a wife and we needed a mother. She seemed different. I remember the day she came. It was evening when they came in. John served them dinner and we all sat around in the living room pretending to be watching our black and white TV. But really, we were studying this stranger in our home. Her finger was really swollen and dad was carefully doing first aid on it. I don't know what she had done to it, it looked like some sort of sting. It was a different side to Dad I must admit. The dad we knew was the serious disciplinarian but here he was gently looking after this woman's finger.

Her name was Dana, we were told, and we were to call her mum. She was in her late twenties and Dad was ten years older than her. Ethan and I, though uncomfortable at first, called her mum, but my stepbrothers never did, never have, and still don't. Ethan and I were happy to have a mother figure again but our stepbrothers didn't like her, and they still don't.

Dana was so young herself. She was the same age as I am today. At the time she had two children of her own, a son and a daughter (they didn't live with us, though). Married to an older man with four little children would have been a daunting task even for a much older, more experienced mother. I could see how overwhelmed she got some days. And sometimes it would be so much for her that she would go visit with her mother or relatives for a week.

A few months later Dana was pregnant. I was excited because ever since I could remember I had prayed that God would give me a sister. I had no idea where babies came from. All I know is that I wanted a sister. In January of 2007 Dana had a baby and it was a girl. I was over the moon! I could not believe that God had answered the prayers of a little girl like me. I was not a Christian but I did believe that God did answer my cry and plea. I was ten at the time and couldn't wait to tell the whole world I had a sister and that I wasn't the only girl anymore!

Dana's presence, however, didn't stop John. For a while he kept doing what he had always been doing. I was so disgusted by the whole situation but, worse still, every time it happened I kept worrying about HIV or being pregnant. I was nine so it was not impossible. He knew I hadn't had my periods yet, so when I raised these concerns he laughed in my face.

Even at that age I loved books and reading. I read every book I got my hands on. I read every news article I could get. I had read of young mothers and those were the years that news of HIV started hitting wavelengths in Kenya, so I knew a lot about that and it scared me. John was still sleeping around the compound with everyone who, in turn, were also sleeping with anyone. Then he would bring all that filth back to the little 9-year-old. I hated him!

At this time I also got a hold of romance novels. They were a comfort as they talked of men who loved the women and swept them off their feet. They were heroes in my sight, and everything John was not. I read the books and dreamed of such a man. It helped me deal with my present situation. The worse my situation was and the worse my emotions got in the many years to come, though, the rougher and meaner the heroes in the romances I read became. The rough men still seemed to get the girl and that was celebrated. John was slowly defining who I thought a man should be or behave. By the time I was 23, this 'innocent' reading past-time had turned into something worse.

I got the courage to go to Dana and I mentioned what had been happening without getting into details. One, because I was embarrassed, but also because I knew if John knew I had told her I would be in trouble. Thinking back, I don't know whether I ever did tell Dad. He is not exactly the most approachable man, so even as a child I didn't know how I could go to him with something as big as what his friend was doing to me. Also, the poison my stepbrothers had fed me about him not being my father made me silent. I didn't want to rock the boat, lest I be kicked out or something. Then one day, as Dana and I were doing our chores at the back of the house, John came out carrying a plastic bag with one trouser and a shirt in it. He said he was taking it to the tailors and he would be back. He never came back and that was the last we ever saw him in our house. Good riddance!

John visited Dad while we were at Grandma Hadassah's about ten years later, in 2007. He greeted me and exclaimed at how much I had grown up, looking me up and down. I was disgusted because for one, he was pretending like he was a long lost uncle who had not seen me in ages, and two, that Dad was still entertaining this man that had defiled me. Why were they still friends? I was hurt by his mere presence and his confidence broke me. I had forgiven him years before but the pain that hit me when I saw him was unbearable. I left the house and left him talking to Dad. I did not come back until I was sure he had left. I have never seen him again.

CHAPTER EIGHT

The abuse had gone on for two years. My childhood stolen from me, my innocence ripped from me. I had been forced to grow up fast. I didn't know how to be a child. I had learned that I was alone in this world and just because I was surrounded by people it did not mean that they really wanted me there. I didn't belong, I wasn't fully accepted. John was gone but the nightmares continued. I still curled up in the corner when I went to sleep. Sometimes I couldn't sleep and those days when I slept in the living room I would watch TV until I could not keep my eyes open. I learnt very quickly that late night TV was not the greatest entertainment, it was often horror movies! I watched a lot of vampire and mass murder movies but then I couldn't sleep as I had nightmares because of what I had watched.

I would cry at night and wonder why my life was what it was. I was still reading and researching whatever caught my attention. I was looking to see whether what I had gone through was normal. I was a very angry, bitter child. I was a friend to all, loved life on the outside but was dying on the inside. In my darkest hours I did consider ending it all. Not just once but many times. I remember one day thinking I should go and walk in the middle of the road and let a car hit me. I was so angry on that day and I know I did leave the house with that intention but didn't quite make it to the road, thank God. I think I ended up in the school field. I calmed down and went back to the house.

My stepbrothers were still not great to me and they were even worse to Dana. I took her side every time and my brothers would mistreat me even more because of it. Even the 9-year-old me knew that Dana, being Dad's wife, was entitled to run the house as she wanted as she was technically our mother and so she was in charge. My stepbrothers didn't get the memo. They did everything she didn't like: play loud music, not letting her watch whatever she wanted, talked back when she asked them to do anything. They criticised everything she did. To them she never did anything right and they still don't think she does. They rejoiced in her misery. The number of times I heard the line 'you are not my mother' is uncountable. This was my life.

Fast forward to 24 August 1999, I had stayed up late studying, as I was in year eight, and we were to sit the national exams in November. My elder brother (the one who used to talk to John) was there. We now had bunk beds and I shared mine with my brother, Ethan, while he shared his with Liam, my immediate older brother. I slept on the top bunk, and he was on the lower on theirs. Ethan and Liam were there too and they had long gone to sleep.

I decided to call it a night and sleep too but my elder brother kept me awake with the most random questions and stories. Every time I dozed off he would ask whether I was awake and then would start talking again. Looking back I figure he was trying to make sure everybody was asleep before saying what he really wanted to say. Next thing I know he is asking me to his bed. I was shocked and really disgusted. He kept asking and asking and no matter how much I said no and that he was my brother, he would reply that we were not related and so that would not matter. In fact he could marry me and it would be okay. I refused but he kept insisting. I cried silently and started praying that he would not rape me. Once again I was made to feel like an object and only good for one thing. He was 16 and I was 12.

The next day I found Dana and quietly told her what had happened. She said she would let Dad know. I never heard of it again and my brother never talked to me like that again. Once again I felt that Dad would not acknowledge what was happening to me right under his roof. He never once asked me if I was okay. Years later he told one of his friends and church elders that this incident and the John incident was a story that Dana and I had made up to make him and his boys look bad.

My peers and I still loved church. We would practise songs so we could go sing at whatever church we could find and would let us. We never stayed in the same church for a long time and stayed longer in the churches that gave us sweets or snacks at Sunday school. The last church we ever went to was a Presbyterian Church. It was a twenty-minute walk from home and somehow our parents let us go by ourselves. We would walk as a group and do the most dangerous things like jumping on the back of vehicles heading our way and hiding., The idea was to see how long the driver would take discover to the little child hanging at the back of their vehicle. Oh, how we made a lot of drivers angry.

In this church we were asked to memorise a lot of Bible passages and every week we would recite them back. When you got it right you would get sweets. Then we would get another verse for the following week, and every week the passages to memorize got longer and longer. The last one we did was:

> *Dear friends in Corinth! We have spoken frankly to you. We have opened our hearts wide. [12]It is not we who have closed our hearts to you; it is you who have closed your hearts to us. [13]I speak now as though you were my children. Show us the same feelings that we have for you. Open your hearts wide!*
>
> *[14]Do not try to work together as equals with unbelievers, for it cannot be done. How can right and wrong be partners? How can light and darkness live together? [15]How can Christ and the devil agree? What does a believer have in common with an unbeliever? [16]How can God's temple come to terms with pagan idols? For we are the temple of the living God! As God himself has said,'I will make my home with my people and live among them. I will be their God, and they shall be my people.'*
>
> *[17]And so the Lord says, 'You must leave them and separate yourselves from them.*
>
> *Have nothing to do with what is unclean, and I will accept you. [18]I will be your father, and you shall be my sons and daughters, says the Lord Almighty.'*
>
> *2 Corinthians 6:11-18(GNT)*

I knew that passage by heart and I listened to one child after the other reciting it at Sunday school. I have to admit though, I didn't really think of the words deeply. I was just happy that I knew the verse and I would get my sweets. And I did! That was the last time we went to that church. Actually it was the last time I went to any church for a couple of years, apart from compulsory church services at school.

The other thing that was special about this church is that they had a big guava tree. It had the biggest, juiciest white guavas. So after church, we would stay back and, after everybody had left, we would be up that tree. We would have a plastic bag ready and we would fill it with guavas. We would then slowly walk home while eating as many guavas as we wanted. And boy didn't we eat a lot of them! Then came the stomach aches and the explaining to our parents why we were not hungry or why we were in pain. In many ways I went to church for all the wrong reasons.

CHAPTER NINE

I was ten when I saw the newspaper article about child prostitution at the Kenyan coast. I remember carefully cutting it out and covering it with sellotape to laminate it, so I could preserve it. I read it over and over again for months. I identified with those girls aged 10 to 13, but they got paid so much, while I only got sweets! Maybe if I went there I could earn enough money to support myself plus I would leave this house where nobody really seemed to want me. So it would be a relief for them and I would get paid a lot for my services.

The article was talking about these young girls making as much as US$100 an hour when they hooked up with foreign tourists. The younger they were, the better. But the report didn't end there. It further said that these European tourists would also get prostitutes for their pets, especially dogs. And for that they would pay a minimum of $200 an hour. That price would also increase depending on what they want the young girl to do to / with the dogs. I was utterly disgusted by it, as the writer of the article clearly was, but I had also realised that that was and had been my life. It offered me financial freedom and freedom from this house. I hated myself and felt the world hated me too. I was the scum of the earth and I deserved this life. I was going to get to the coast somehow and someday. I didn't care about the logistics. I was going to run away and that gave me hope and something to look forward to.

The following year my brother, Elijah, came to stay with us when he had finished high school. Elijah is my father's first-born from his first marriage / relationship. He is a Christian and had been through high school. Dad was not happy about that. In fact, it was because of Elijah's conversion that I didn't go to church anymore.

Dad saw himself as a Christian, a Quaker. In fact he taught Christian Religious Education and he knows the Bible more than most people I know. However, he rarely went to a church and I had noticed that since I was a child. He sent us to church with the maids or by ourselves but he didn't go.

I remember one of the times he did go to church, and he, John and a few others went out to the front when the pastor asked who wanted to be born again. They were asked to put their hands up and say a prayer and at the end of the prayer, they said, 'I am born again.' I particularly remember this day because they had had their hands up for a while and ended up putting their hands on their heads. I looked on amused as they prayed but also hopeful that this meant that John would change and leave me alone. But that didn't happen. Nothing changed.

Elijah, on the other hand, did become a Born Again Christian and his life did change to reflect that. He prayed, preached, read the Bible and went for missions. It became his life. Dad was angry because, according to him, that was the reason he was failing his exams. So one evening, while Elijah was still in high school, Dad angrily told us that he *never* wants any of us to say we are Born Again Christians. We could be Christians after university, he told us, but not when we are still in school or in his house, as that was just an excuse to fail exams.

To be fair to Elijah, he had not had a great start in school and consequently he didn't do well. He wasn't very academic either. The rest of us went to a private school in Kera, while he moved from public school to school in the country. He also lived in different places so his home life was not the most stable. Even as a child, hearing Dad talking like that, I wondered at how unfair it was on Elijah. What chance did he have to achieve the academic excellence Dad was demanding?

I learnt from that age that sharing or having a faith was not permitted in that house so I stopped pursuing it all together. That was hard because church had become something I looked forward to, not because I understood what was going on, but because it had become my escape and I saw genuinely happy people there. I often wondered what made them so happy and full of joy. Part of me also wondered whether they were faking it, as I had been doing for years, and that made me sceptical to the realness of their joy. I wanted to hang out with them but not pursue what they had.

The months Elijah stayed with us he talked a lot about the word of God and he taught me (or tried to teach me) a lot about God. For the first time in my life religious education was not just a classroom subject but was alive in my house. Even so I just listened politely because I respected him being my eldest brother. At the end of his stay he wrote down so many verses. He gave them to me and said I should learn them by heart. He also said that when he came back, he would quiz me on the verses.

The only verse I knew by heart by then was John 3:16. I didn't remember a single verse or chapter that I had learnt for church in the previous years. Those were crammed just for the sweets and the recognition, not really for remembering purposes. And now, here were more for me to learn. The first one I learnt was Psalm 63:1:

> O God, you are my God, and I long for you. My whole being desires you; like a dry, worn-out, and waterless land, my soul is thirsty for you. (GNT)

That verse made me really think of my life, and I think made me realise just how empty my life was! I wondered whether David had experienced what I was. My life was dry and was parched. I needed water but not the usual kind. I was thirsty but water would not quench it. I definitely knew that I wasn't seeking God earnestly like the psalmist was. I knew I had not thirsted after God and my whole being belonged to me and not to him. Then I got another verse just like that one in Psalms 42:1–3,

> ¹As the deer pants for streams of water, so my soul pants for you, my God.
> ²My soul thirsts for God, for the living God.
> When can I go and meet with God?
> ³My tears have been my food day and night, while people say to me all day long,
> 'Where is your God?' (NIV)

Oh how true was the part that says tears had been my food! Where was my God? Is there a God, and if he was there, then he was really unfair to let me go through the things I had. But I couldn't tell him that, I was afraid of God. Perhaps, if I dared challenge him, he would strike me right where I stood. The God I knew and heard about was a very mean God who sent people to hell, seemed always angry, and demanded to always be feared. I had better not do anything to draw any attention to myself. I felt so small, insignificant and had convinced myself and believed God didn't care about me. But if I even shifted my weight from one foot to the other in his presence, and he noticed me, he would snuff my life out for the bother! By ignoring him I had silently decided I wanted nothing to do with him. He was too busy for me anyway, so I had to run my own life.

Some of the other verses included, 'No one can please God without faith.' (Hebrews 11:6 NIV). 'I am the way, the truth, and the life, no one comes to the Father except through me' (John 14:6 NIV). 'The devil comes to kill steal and destroy but I have come to give you life and life in its fullness' (John 10:10 NIV) among many others.

I did learn the verses though and he did quiz me about them. I was saying these words over and over that I actually started thinking about my life and I started wondering whether the God I thought I knew was the true God. At the same time I had decided this was the year to run away and start a new life far away. My plan was to go up country with the family for Christmas and then when we get back into the city, before we catch the bus home, I would disappear in the crowd and board a bus headed to the coast. It was a fearful thought but I had convinced myself it needed to be done, for I knew I was a burden to those around me. But slowly, without realising it, my heart of stone was melting.

CHAPTER TEN

During Christmas of 1998 we were up country at Grandma Hadassah's. We went to visit her every December. I had decided this was going to be the last year. When we got back to Kera, I would disappear into the crowd and go my way, as I had planned for two years. This was my goodbye to my father's people. I was going to sit tight for these next few weeks.

On this Christmas day I was up very early, went to the river to fetch water as usual, and did my usual chores. I then had a shower and put on my Christmas outfit (we got a new outfit for Christmas every year, everyone seemed to have one). My cousin, Nora, and I hit the road to spend the day walking around.

Christmas was the only day in the year that we ever got any pocket money from our parents. And this one was no exception. Dad gave me Ksh 20 (approximately AUD 0.40). That was a lot of money for me because it is all we got all year. Plus, we could buy four full-sized sugar canes. Yes, I did say sugar cane. We loved walking around just chewing sugarcane, watching dances, listening to Christmas memory verses and Christmas choir competitions. We also loved analysing the fashion of the season and got hours of entertainment doing so, never realising how ridiculous we also looked to others.

This particular day was really hot, so we were tired and hot. We had hardly spent our pocket money on anything, mostly because we couldn't make up our minds. We decided to rest on a bench under a tree in the marketplace. There was a church that had set up a crusade there and preaching was going on. Nora explained that the church was the church Elijah went to when he was up country. He was there too, not that he had seen us.

There was a visiting pastor from Uganda. Ugandans hardly speak Swahili. Their official language is English, but their national language is Buganda. Kenya's official language is English, while national language is Swahili. Here in the village, very few spoke English. Most spoke Swahili and the local language. So the preacher had to use English and got a young man who spoke all three languages to interpret. It was clear that this young man had been brought up in the city. I was so entertained listening to him speaking the local language with a twang and sometimes not even knowing how to interpret some of the words the preacher said. Sometimes he would end up using the same English word or try explaining the word. He was a good-looking guy, so he got my attention for that too. Nora and I just sat there listening, daydreaming, and laughing at some of the things he did say. I have no recollection of what was preached that day. I don't even remember the name of the handsome interpreter.

Next thing we know, the preacher calls the children to go forward to be born again. All the kids run forward. Nora and I were left sitting and could feel the eyes on us. We felt so out of place that we too stood up and to the front we went. Well, I knew what being born again was in theory because that was all Elijah talked about. I had also seen dad go through it but didn't see a difference in him, so to me it didn't make sense.

We did say a prayer and then we were ushered into a room where we were given a piece of paper to write our names. I remember I was the first one to write my name down. The other kids were so shy and seemed hesitant. I didn't see what I had to lose, so I wrote it down and then the rest followed. The young man who was with us then asked if we had a question; of course I did have questions!

'So now that we are born again. What next?' I asked. 'What does it mean? What are we to do?' I asked.

He was amused. He replied, saying it meant we were new creations and that God had forgiven our sins and we are now children of God. He said now as God's children we should spend time reading the Bible, going to church and praying.

'Is that all?' I asked.

Well it did sound very easy, so I purposed to do it. Maybe it would make a difference in my life. We went home for Christmas dinner soon after. Elijah was excited that his sister was now a Christian.

The days that followed I went wherever my brother and the church went to minister after doing my chores. The visiting pastor was still around for the week and he was going around to homes and doing a few more open-air meetings around the area. I was surprised my dad and mum let me go because they would never allow me to leave the house to go anywhere usually. But they hardly questioned where I was going during this week. I had decided to give this Christian thing a week to prove life-changing because come what may, I was leaving in the New Year. Following this preacher everywhere was my way of observing Christianity in action.

During the week many more people were born again and many were sick but were healed when he prayed for them. Faith was built. I watched on.

The dreaded Christmas holidays had turned into a season of rebirth. Mum was buried on Christmas Eve between 1 and 3 p.m. in 1993, and I was born again on Christmas day around the same hours. These are two major events that took place five years apart. Today Christmas is a bittersweet season for me, a time to mourn a mum I never got to know and a time to celebrate Christ who change my life from the inside out and who assures me every day that one day, I will get to spend time with my mum again.

First of January 1999, we were in the church for the New Year service. It was the last day for the Ugandan pastor. I had on long pants, something very brave to wear up country back in the day. Girls in pants were frowned upon. Only prostitutes and loose Nairobi girls wore them. I had them on in church! We sang praises, we worshipped, we listened, he preached. In the middle of his sermon, he stops and looks at me.

'Young girl, stand up,' he says pointing at me.

I was terrified. Oh dear, I will be shamed for wearing something so scandalous! There I was eleven years old, red ears from embarrassment, standing up in the middle of an overflowing church! Every eye was on me.

'Everyone, look at this young girl,' he continued, increasing my embarrassment. 'She has been with us everywhere we have gone this week, quietly watching us. Young girl', he said, now addressing me,

'God says if you trust in him and give him your whole life, he will make all things right and your name great.' (Note: Not word for word for what he said but something along those lines.)

I was then asked to sit down and he kept preaching. I didn't hear anything else he said after that. In fact, the rest of the service was a blur. God had a word for me? God thought I was worth a thought? Really? Nobody knew I was running away the next day! How did this pastor think to tell me that? Was that really God? Would he really make my name great if I trusted him? Was running away showing trust in God? Why now? What was I going to do? What did trusting God look like? Who was I that he spared just a few minutes for me? Oh, so many questions but no answers.

Over the years, a lot more people have told me things that have reminded me that God does care for little, insignificant me. Some have been so specific and personal that they can only be from God, as the people who spoke to me did not know of what was going on in my life, and some things I had not even shared with those closest to me. I guess it is God's way of reminding me that he is real and he does care even for the smallest detail of my life.

Nova and I headed home after the service. We didn't talk much about what had happened but when we got home Elijah, who had also been in the congregation, had already told everyone what had happened at church and what the pastor had said.

The next day we took our packed bags, boarded a bus, and started our seven-hour journey back home—a lot of time to think about my escape or not escape. I kept putting off thinking about it but I knew this was my one chance to get away, otherwise it would be too late. I would be 12 going on 13 next year. The article had said the kids were between 10–12 years old. I was going to be 12 this year and therefore, my 'prime' years were gone. I would probably be considered too old. I had already wasted my opportunity the last two years. Was I going to let this one go too? But the pastor's words always came back to me, 'If you trust God…'

We got to Kera and as I waited for Dad and Mum to get the bags I hesitated for a moment. This was it. It was time to make a decision. I looked around slowly as my mind turned. Everything around me seemed to have been on slow motion.

'I would trust God,' I decided. He had promised to make everything better. I was going to trust that. We went home and that was my first lesson in God's timing. He is never early and never late, he is always on time.

What followed was almost two decades of tears, laughter, and hope. God did and is still fulfilling that promise, but not in the way I wanted him to and often not in the timeframe I wanted him to (those of you in Christ know exactly what I mean). Things didn't get easier actually. In human eyes it got worse! But looking back I can see how all things work together for God's good (Romans 8:28 NIV). God is in control indeed.

CHAPTER ELEVEN

First order of business was to hide the born again part from Dad. Second was to look for a way I would grow as a Christian because going to church was out of the question. Suddenly the world was not safe according to my dad. The same dad who let us walk to a church far away when we were much younger now would not let us leave the compound.

One day, playing around with his radio (the only radio we had in the house), I discovered Family FM—a Christian radio station. I also realised there was preaching everyday on television and lots of other Christian programs like 700 Club, CBN, and many others. I had my Bible and so I started listening, watching, and reading. I was so fascinated with the Bible stories, the testimonies I heard, the music I listened to over the next two years. I felt loved and accepted by not those around me every day but by God himself. I was full of joy no matter the storms going on around me, and there were quite a few of those.

First of all, the fighting between my step-mum and brothers did not cease. My stepbrothers had not stopped reminding me that I wasn't one of them. I still missed Mum and would cry, asking why she had to leave me. It was a hard year.

That same year I suggested to my class to have prayers every day, ten minutes before quitting time. We would have someone read a Bible verse and another to pray. We also started a Bible study with my friends at home. I remember we would all get our Bibles and sit outside together, sing a few songs and study together, pray, and then get on with playing. Our parents would find us praying and reading the Bible together when they came home from work, and they would be so impressed and would encourage us to keep doing it.

The year went by very quickly, and soon it was 28 June 1999. I was turning twelve. I didn't celebrate my birthday, as Dad was convinced I was born in July and not June. He later changed all my certificates to read July but I always knew in my heart my birthday was in June. I waited the month to officially celebrate my birthday in July. Now I just joke that I have two birthdays; June being when I was actually born and July when I was officially recognised as being born. I have a whole month for hibernation.

On the evening of the 28 July, I was walking home from home when I felt something strange. I rushed home and realised my period had started. I was so excited to see it. I don't think there's anyone who was as excited as I was to see blood. I never thought I would ever have them because though it had been a few years I still had an irrational fear that I was pregnant after being raped for the two years. Another fear I carried for years was that I had HIV, but that's another story.

Anyway, I went and shared with Mum the great news, and she didn't seem as excited as I was. Thankfully we had had a few classes in school on what to do and had been given a few sanitary towels. I used them. But when the next period came I didn't have anything to use and Dad could not afford to buy any more. Mum showed me how to fold up a few cloths, using them and then washing them. For the next two years I used pieces of bedsheets that I would cut up from old sheets and sometimes I would cut a piece of foam mattress and wrap the piece with the pieces of old bedsheets and use that. Every few hours I would have to change it and then wash by hand and hang to dry. I couldn't hang it outside, of course, because it was not really the kind of thing that you would want Dad or your brothers to see, let alone neighbours. So I had to hang them in my room, under my towel hidden from view. When I went to high school sanitary towels were part of the requirements, so I did have them in high school.

I had longed for a mother that I could talk to until midnight or cuddle with in silence. I longed for a father who would embrace me and make me feel safe. I got none of that. My relationship with Dana, though civil enough, was not one of a mother and her daughter. It was more like roommates who had reached a truce and decided to live together in peace. I tried once too many times to tell her things but they would end up in Dad's ear and sometimes I would get in trouble. I learnt quite fast that I would not be able to share or ask her anything.

My relationship with Dad, on the other hand, was one of fear. He was a provider and nothing else, so he was not approachable either. The sister I had longed for was too young and therefore I never enjoyed that kind of relationship either. My brothers, on the other hand, were also like roommates. I couldn't really talk to them either. We were so many in the house yet I was all alone.

What I learnt in my life, I have learnt from observing, from imagination, from books, and from other people's parents. I was never close enough to anyone to ask any questions that a young lady would want to ask, but I learnt how to research on my own to get the answers I sought.

I heard it once said by a very close friend that I was out to steal her mother and she wanted me to know that her mum never be my mother. Of course I do know she will never be my mother and I also know the friend said so to hurt me. We had a disagreement and are no longer as close as we once were. In my latter teenage years and early adulthood I had become very close to her mother. She was the first woman who treated me like a daughter and spoke to me like a mother. Consequently I call her mother. She and I became so close that the day I announced my engagement. Instead of Dad asking Dana to talk sense to me, he called this lady to talk to me. She called me and we talked a while. She asked me the questions a mother asks a daughter when she decides to marry. She asked to meet Zane as soon as possible. And when she did on Christmas Day of 2010 she asked Zane all the hard questions a concerned mother asks her soon to be son-in-law. Zane calls her mum too now and she loves Zane like a son.

Dana didn't ask a question, she didn't even speak to Zane much. Dad didn't either. All he said was he was not handing his daughter over to a fellow child and therefore wanted to meet his parents. I know I cannot take her from my friend, and my intention had and will never be to take anyone's mum away. I just longed for a mother and she filled that role for the last ten years I have known her.

I was alone when my heart was broken or when I was sad for no reason or when I just wanted someone older and wiser to speak to. Even having just turned twelve I was alone and celebrated by myself this big step of becoming a woman.

Dear daughters, when I see people take their parents for granted and the relationships they have with them, it breaks my heart. And when they take little things for granted or complain about how life is hard, I think of how ungrateful they are. Here I was, in what would be considered a middle class family in Kenya, and we couldn't afford sanitary towels. Don't take whatever you have for granted. I pray you will always have a higher perspective of life than your immediate surroundings. Whatever you have is a blessing from God, be thankful for it. I pray you will always put yourself in another's shoe before complaining, making fun of, or thinking you are entitled. And most of all I pray you will not take the relationship you have with your parents, grandparents, sisters, uncles, or aunties lightly either. Treasure what God has blessed you with, for there are many more who cry, yearn, and pray for it but never get it.

My mum, Dana, started going away a lot and so I became the cook and cleaner in the home when she was not around. That meant I wasn't playing with my friends as much anymore. I made the most of the time I had with them though. It was difficult being in charge of a house of five with four of them being boys, especially teenage boys and a man. I had to cook for ten because they were big eaters but there was not much food to cook. I had to be very creative. Sometimes Dad would not leave enough money and I would be out in the garden harvesting the new grown kale from what mostly looked like sticks. I would then cook it with lots of water to give the illusion of there being a lot.

We were not rich by any stretch of the imagination. We got by. We were the only family that didn't have a colour television in the estate, had no VCR or a fridge. We had the bare minimal. We cooked on charcoal, *jikos*, or used kerosene stoves. We hardly ate meat because we couldn't afford it. And when we did have meat, the pieces had to be counted to make sure we all got an equal share (my stepbrothers hated this and still hold it against our step-mum, but truth be told they would be the first to complain if one person got more pieces than they did). If we were lucky to get eggs Mum would mix it with spinach to bulk it up. None of us really liked this combination but we had no choice but to eat it. We hardly ever had new clothes. Dad had only one pair of shoes, four trousers, and four shirts for work. I remember him wearing the shoes until they had holes in them and even then he would have them repaired., But he would buy us a pair of shoes before he would buy his own.

We got teased a lot because we clearly had nothing compared with others, and we were four of us living with Dad at the time. The teasing unfortunately didn't come from our peers but some of their parents. I remember my brothers and me overhearing a conversation between the headmistress who also lived in the compound with her grandson (who was one of our friends) and one of the other parents. They were talking in Kikuyu, a different language to ours—not realising we actually understood and spoke the language. They were asking each other 'what all those children are for?'—referring to dad. They couldn't understand why dad had so many children. They continued to discuss how they couldn't understand why we were so many. My brothers and I wondered why it bothered them so much. We had never gone begging at their house or anything like that.

CHAPTER TWELVE

Dad was hard-worker and like any good parent wanted the very best for his children—part of that was taking us to good private schools. So in many ways we could be considered rich because Dad prioritised education and knowledge over luxury. He worked a full time job as a teacher and did a lot of tuition on the side so we could have the best education. That meant we hardly ever saw Dad and when he was home, he was emotionally and physically tired; therefore very irritable.

His father before him also emphasised education for a better life, and he too sacrificed everything for his children to go to school. My dad would walk for kilometres with a metal box, which contained all his school gear, to go to school. My grandfather experienced colonialism and he wanted a different life for his children. So dad and his siblings went to school whether they wanted to or not. When they were home for the school holidays they had to find jobs, like working in people's farms harvesting tea leaves, so as to help Granddad pay the Kshs 0.90 tax that the British had put on their land. This was even though it was their ancestral land! The tax was a hefty sum for a people that never used the money system and especially for people who were used to ruling themselves) The colonizers made the locals pay tax on the land they had owned for generations.

A story is told of how Dad, his parents and the older siblings would be out working all day and the youngest boy would be left at home to cook the afternoon meal so that the hungry, tired workers would have something to eat when they got home. Nora tells me a story of the youngest uncle serving raw tea, a concept I never understood, to the annoyance of the workers who were tired having toiled all day. But they still ate and drank what he served. That became a joke even now in adulthood—the only person I know who burns black tea or serves it raw. My grandparents also had a little tea farm and tea is a big part of my dad's culture so they were all supposed to be tea experts. Luhyas know good tea and bad tea.

Dad didn't like the colonizers just as I suspect his dad before him hadn't. He taught history in school and one thing he said over and over again was that we should remember that the white man was not superior to us and just because they say to do something does not mean we should. I got the impression that he didn't want much to do with them. Fair enough though, the colonizers had caused a lot of pain and chaos during his childhood and this shaped his world view on westerners. I think he was out to prove to himself and to others that he too can achieve what they, the colonizers, deemed important and go even further. Years later, I brought home a white fiancé. The move, though not objected, caught him off guard.

One of Dad's favourite things to say was that he got to college and therefore he was going to work harder and push us even more to make sure we went a step further than he did and get a degree. He hoped we would make sure our children earnt a Ph.D! This became his ultimate goal no matter what else went wrong around him.

Dad didn't seem to be lucky in love. He had two relationships before my mum, Sarah. Elijah was a child of the first that ended years before he met my mum. He then met another woman. They had two sons before that relationship ended bitterly. To date they do not get along. Then came my mum with two children, and she passed away. Then Dana is the last lady who is still with him for twenty years and counting. He was never married to two women at the same time.

I have to hand it to Dad for never denying his own children and looking after all his children. He is a man who took responsibility for his actions and this is to be applauded, especially in this present generation filled with fatherless children and many men with children with different women and possibly taking care of none.

Dad had a favourite chair in the house and when he was in the house the remote was his. We would watch what he wanted, watched or listen to what he wanted to listen to on the radio. I clearly remember how Dad would come in and find us watching TV or hanging out in the lounge room. Then, as if on cue, we would get up from the eldest to the youngest to hide in our room. To me it was like the scene of the woman caught in adultery who was brought to Jesus, and Jesus had told the crowd let him with no sin to cast the first stone. The story says that they started going away one by one. I have always imagined them going away starting with the oldest to the youngest, perhaps because the older one probably has more sins because of a longer life. So we left in the same fashion from the oldest, and then the next would wait a few seconds and leave, and so on. Other times he would be coming through the front door and we would be going through the back. We did fear our dad, that's for sure. Nobody wanted to be there when he lost his temper.

I remember one day in year three when my religious education teacher happened to ask me what tribe I came from. I confidently said I was from my mum's tribe. She could not understand because Dad was from a different one and my immediate older brother, Liam, who was in the same class insisted he was from Dad's tribe. Even at that age I had never felt like I was part of their culture. I never felt at home when we went up country and often wondered why I just felt like a foreigner in their land. Now I do know why I did feel like a foreigner. I was a foreigner.

I didn't think much of it after the lesson as the teacher seemed to have moved on. Little did I know she would raise the issue in the staffroom to Dad in front of other teachers. Dad was embarrassed and Dad hates embarrassment. Consequently he was angry, and I was on the other end of that anger. He came home and gave me one of the biggest lectures I have ever had and told me that if I ever told anyone else I was not from his family I would be in even bigger trouble. I never did it again, and that night I quietly cried to myself. I felt as though I had been asked to ignore part of who I was and to be embarrassed about that part of me.

To be sincere, Dad didn't discriminate among us. I think if one took a closer look he favoured me more than the others. He often called to send me, to talk to me about random things, trusted me with file and information that I don't think my brothers even know exist to date. I will never forget the day Dad called me to speak to me in his room. He had been unwell and had been in bed for a couple of days. I think he was just bored so he called me in and, as usual, started talking about random things. I was about 15 at the time and we were home for school holidays.

After a long chat I realised that I might be there for a long while longer, so I sat down on the floor beside his bed. Suddenly, he stopped talking. He then said this is Swahili, 'I am so sorry I am not the father I should be to you, but I am trying my best. The sacrifices I make I make for you. I am sorry I cannot buy you the things 15-year-olds like. I am sorry I can't afford the latest fashion or take you to places.' He stopped, and I looked up at him wondering what he would say next. I was surprised at what I saw in his eyes—tears. Now, for those who know my dad know he is not a very emotional person. In fact we often wonder whether he had any other feelings apart from anger. But here he was fighting the tears in his eyes.

'I don't want you to tell people you did not have a father,' and then he paused. 'Who cared,' he continued. 'I do care, and I am trying my best.' I believed him, and this is the first time ever I am sharing that conversation.

That single day was the most revealing day of who Dad is since I have known him. It is also the only time since and before that I witnessed Dad's vulnerability. He was trying and even though he failed once too many times, I do believe he was trying.

Dad's nickname among my paternal cousins was *Vitisho*, which is translated to 'threats' in English. Only difference is his were not idle threats. He disciplined all us kids including his siblings' kids. And the same way we ran from him is the same way my cousins did too!

Outsiders saw a very different man to who we knew and a lot of people would highly praise him and tell me how lucky I was for having such a great father. He was a kind, generous man who loved kids. He was patient, yet firm. A great teacher and friend. He would easily give you the shirt on his back if he thinks you need it more. We saw this side too at home and continue to see it even now, but we also saw the dark side of him. Dad has taught me a lot of things about sharing the much or little I have. His hand has always been open to others. I remember asking if friends could come stay over when they were in Nairobi, or if they had nowhere to go. Dad's response was they could, even though we did not have enough to eat ourselves. He would say it was good for said friends to see how we live, and they too would get to experience it. So if we did not have anything to eat, they would not eat either.

Over the years we have had a lot of people stay with us. Even after high school we have had our friends and other relatives stay with Dad and Mum for days, weeks and months, even when we ourselves were not there. The longest was one of my brother's friends who stayed with them for a year, post university, as he was looking for a job. When he got one and found a house, he moved out with bedding and other things to the horror of Mum. Dad was unmoved by the blatant theft. He just simply said that they were material things and God would provide others even though he didn't have spare ones. Material things and the loss of them did not move him much. He would be upset about it but not so much as to make a big fuss about it. Relationships came first, things second.

He was not embarrassed about his financial status and he taught me never to let money define me. It was good to have it and to use it wisely on things that mattered and were eternal, but integrity, morals and a clear conscience is what should matter most. He continually taught us both in words and deed. And for that, I truly admire him.

These two sides of him truly baffled and confused me growing up. Half the time I didn't know which Dad I had in the house on a particular day or hour. In hindsight, it was a good thing because it meant I did not put him on a pedestal and expect him to be a saint. Most things he did or did not do did not surprise me because even as a young child I realised he was just human.

I have met a lot of people in my life who do not speak to their parents or hate their parents so much for things their parents have done to them or to others. I feel sorry for the parents and the unforgiving child because I realise that the children probably idolised and put them on a pedestal but the moment they fail the child closes that door and totally loses respect for the parent. They forget that they, too, will one day be parents themselves, or are parents in the present day, and their children will probably do the same to them when they fail.

Parents are humans and they do fall, make wrong choices, and do silly things. Not forgiving them for this means carrying a burden all your life or their children doing the same thing they have done to their own parents. When you let anger, hate and bitterness rule your every waking hour, it will finally consume you. And when you think about what and how your parents let you down over and over again, chances are you will end up doing what they did or even worse. Or your children will end up doing to you what you did to your own parents. What goes around comes around, even in the parenting world, generation after generation.

I have seen a man who blames his dad for abandoning him as a child. Then he kicks his seven-month pregnant wife and they lose the baby. He then abandons her with their other children and leaves her to bury the baby alone. He doesn't even know the burial site of his daughter.

I have seen a girl who thought poorly of her mum, who was a single mother, and could not keep a man. She also ended up being a single mother, going from relationship to relationship.

I have met a random stranger as I was dropping my eldest at preschool, who stopped us and, with tears in her eyes, said she wishes her daughter would at least forgive her so she could be at peace instead of holding on to the anger and bitterness. The daughter has moved to a different state because she wants nothing to do with her mother. The stranger who stopped me was afraid her daughter would turn into her and make the same choices, and her children in turn would walk away, as she had done to her mother who had been begging for forgiveness. She was also in pain because she was missing the chance to see and meet her grandchildren who are the same age as my girls.

I have talked to a few parents whose children are not speaking to them for a mistake they did and choices they made. The parents' pain and regret is apparent and they mostly tell me that they wish the child would forgive them even if they never speak to each other again. That bitterness and unforgiveness will destroy their children's life in and of itself. No parent wants to see their child suffer, in pain and self-destructing. There are indeed many examples around us of people who have chosen not to forgive their parents for bad choices they had made and consequently they are walking in their parents' shoes (or worse) a few years down the line. You cannot expect forgiveness when you refuse to forgive!

This is the position I hold with Dad. I will honour my parents as the Bible tells me to, I will love them and serve them, as the Bible instructs me to. I don't agree sometimes with actions taken and decisions made but that does not mean I will not forgive and move on. Anger, bitterness, and unforgiveness breed the same issues in my own life. I would not want to be like the dark side of Dad so I will take the wonderful lessons I learnt from him and discard and forgive the wrongs done to me under his protection.

CHAPTER THIRTEEN

One day, I was called into the house by Dad to make him a cup of tea. We had just had a good afternoon of playing and laughing and I wasn't impressed when Dad called me inside. I had been sensing some hostility from my friends but I had not thought much of it. I didn't think it was serious.

As I was serving Dad I saw one of my friends running from my bedroom window laughing. I was curious and so was dad, so I went into my bedroom to see what was going on. Right there on the floor was a folded paper. I was sure that had just been dropped in, as I had never seen it before. I opened it. They were two letters in it. One was written in red pen. My eye was immediately drawn to the bottom of that one. In big red letters the words, 'We hate you!' were written. I quickly scanned the rest of the letter, tears stinging my eyes. It was a list of thing each of the kids hated about me. I was heartbroken I couldn't keep reading it. I ran to Dad and showed him what it was.

Dad put them away. He was furious! Furious that the kids were brave enough to run through our garden to drop off such a hateful letter. Furious because they were not brave enough to tell me in my face or even knock on the front door and hand it to me like respectful children. Furious because of what was written in it and the pain it was causing me. He called their parents. The mothers came and what ensued was a shouting match, with Dad angrily banging on our dining room table. The kids had come with their parents and we were made to sit there and listen to it all. That was beyond torture. The kids were looking at me making faces while their parents were defending their actions and telling Dad just how bad I really was based on what their children had told them. Even then, as their children made faces and snide remarks in my face, they said and did nothing. This emboldened them even more.

One of the parents asked to be shown the letter and they all read it. When the last one got it, she tore it into pieces saying that I was also mean to their child and that I probably deserved it. 'Anyway, it is just children being children and we should let them be,' she said. I couldn't believe my ears. The parents were worse than the children! No wonder the kids were acting as they were. I was rubbish in their eyes, and they didn't care what happened to me.

That meeting ended with no resolution. Dad told me not to worry and to know I didn't have to be friends with them or play with them. But I was trapped. Our house was at the end of the street. I had to pass their houses to go anywhere. Plus, who else would I play with? I didn't know any other kids, so my life of seclusion and loneliness began. School days were fine as I could interact with other kids from school (the school was a boarding / day school, and we lived in the school compound), but weekends and holidays were really hard as I had to stay indoors alone.

The next few weeks were really hard. The kids played and talked to my brothers like normal, but wanted nothing to do with me. The only one who talked to me was my best friend's sister, Maya. She would come to our house and sit with me and we would talk. She would also help me with cooking and chores. I really appreciated that company. It lasted until her sister told her to leave me alone or else, and next thing I know I was alone again. Maya stopped talking to me too.

One day, they sent one of the younger boys, Steven, to call me. They wanted to talk to me, they said. I remember being excited as I thought they were going to apologise. I went, naively. They took me to the farthest point from my house and next thing I know, my boyfriend, Caleb, had brought out all the gifts I had ever bought him and other things we had shared over the years. He pretended to give them back to me saying that he wanted nothing to do with me. He then 'accidentally' dropped them all in a muddy puddle. He did this as he made fun of me. I wondered what he shared with everybody about me.

Tears stung my eyes at that moment. I kept trying to push them away and bravely stood there as about seven kids looked on and laughed at me. Caleb kept talking and pushing the books and other things around in the muddy puddle. I slowly turned around, hands across my chest and walked away, head down, with laughter and ridicule behind me following me all the way home. I cried when I got home.

Maya came over to check on me. I talked to her for a while and then went into the house and got out all the letters, gifts, photos, and anything else that was Caleb-related. Maya and I made a bonfire. That was it. That chapter of my life had been closed and would never be opened again. I vowed to myself that no man would ever make a fool of me again. But that's not how life works.

One day I had been sent to the shops. I, of course, had to pass their houses to get to the gate but as soon as they saw me, they followed me, calling me names and making rude sounds. I reached the gate and couldn't even get to where I was going. I decided to go back to the house. The same thing happened as I was walking back. The loudest in the group was my then best friend. Thankfully her mum was coming home and had witnessed a bit of what was going on. I approached her and pleaded with her to ask her daughter to leave me alone. She did and then asked us to follow her to her house. Immediately after she turned her back on us my best friend spat on my face. I immediately let her mum know. She casually turned to her daughter and said, 'Oh, that's not nice,' and kept walking.

We followed her as her daughter and the other kids kept calling me names and laughing all the way to her house. She said nothing! We got to her house and she proceeded to give us a 'lecture' on friendship and forgiveness, and reminded us that we had been good friends. She then made her daughter and I apologise to each other and asked the other kids to do the same. I did sincerely apologise, even though I still had no idea what I had done to be bullied. I also didn't think this apology session was serious because of how the mum had reacted to the spitting incident, the name calling all the way to her house, and even in her house as she spoke. To me she was doing this just for show. This was cemented by the way she and the other parents had spoken to my dad a few weeks earlier when all this started. To me this bullying started right from the parents.

Six years later one of those kids, Chloe, Sam's elder sister, called me out of the blue. We caught up and talked for a while. She is the only one out of the group to have ever apologised for what happened.

Another day she called me asking to visit and she said that Caleb wanted to come along too. I had not seen nor spoken to him since that painful day six years before. They came. When I saw Caleb I remember thinking to myself, 'What in the heavens did I see in this boy?' He was shorter than me, had unruly dreadlocks, and the whole time he was at my house visiting me he spent on the computer listening to gangster rap and hip-hop!

As Chloe and I talked, she turned to me and said, 'I can't believe I was envious of you and Caleb! If I knew he would turn out this way, I would have never even entertained the thought!' We laughed as I confirmed I was glad he had broken it off with me too.

A few days after that visit I got a text from Caleb saying that he had been glad to catch up with me and it had brought back very many happy memories of our relationship. He wondered whether there was a chance to get back together. To say I was shocked would be an understatement!

Fast forward to sixteen years in 2016 as I was writing this book. I decided to ask my best friend, Lucy, back then what all that conflict was about. We had recently reconnected but that had never been discussed. For the purposes of this book I thought I should ask one of the leaders of the whole messy ordeal what it was all about for me to get an understanding of it too, as I still have no idea.

Lucy had no recollection of the incident, especially the spitting part. She was sad that I had carried it around all my life. I pointed out that I was the one bullied and therefore I would remember it. It affected me as a person. It destroyed my self-esteem and confidence. I needed to understand my part in the conflict so I can understand their actions. She did not think it was important, and pointed out that all she remembers is that we were best of friends and I was into going to church. After I quoted the letter that was written to me, the words they spoke, and the spitting on my face, she was shocked and asked for forgiveness.

The above conversation made me learn something else about humanity. We don't see things that have not happened to us as big deals. We belittle other people's experiences because we have not felt it for ourselves. Empathy, I have discovered, is a gift that many do not possess. This 'little fight' lasted two years but my best friend at the time thought it was a matter of days and doesn't have a recollection of any of it. Consequently she doesn't understand why I remember it. To her it shouldn't matter and I shouldn't even remember it. It didn't happen to her. I'm sure the same will be said of this book.

Most people (my family included) will ask 'Why now?' and 'Why should it matter because it happened so long ago?'. This, I feel, is the excuse we give others and ourselves so that we do not deal with our own past skeletons. We try to move on and not deal with past experiences but these experiences do affect our present and our future. Think of your own life, what are you ignoring in your past that you do not want to deal with? What are you trying to call bygones that are still affecting you today? If you do not deal with it, it will show up again in the future. When it does, it will be a bigger issue that it was when you first experienced it. Pain, bitterness, and unresolved issues are like a cancer within us. They keep growing until we seek to deal with them.

It doesn't matter to those who have not experienced it but those who share a similar experience understand the burden that comes with it. It is a living reality in our lives. There's nothing I appreciate less than being told it doesn't matter, because that cheapens and dismisses me and my life. It is choosing to ignore one of the biggest parts of my life and what makes me into who I am. Though my experiences do not define me, they shape and mould me and my action and reaction in life.

These events shaped me into who I am and by rejecting them I reject part of myself. To understand Purity, one must understand the stories and circumstances that shaped her into who she is and the same applies to everyone else. Our stories matter. Your stories, whether big or small, long or short, painful or joyful, matter. They make you into you.

CHAPTER FOURTEEN

As all this drama was going on with my friends outside, I noticed a suitcase in my dad's bedroom that was always locked. I knew what was in it, we all did, but we were never allowed to look in it. It had a few things that belonged to my mother, Sarah. I went to Dad and asked him if he could allow me to look through it. He agreed and I was thrilled. I was twelve years old.

I opened the box. There were photo albums and books in it. For the first time since Mum died I saw a photo of her. I remember touching her face in the photos with tears streaming down my face. I had lots of questions. I missed her, and oh, how I longed for her and to talk to her. How I longed to be seated with her singing our song. I even missed her disciplining. I just missed her and who she had been. I wondered whether I would have been as lonely as I was now if she was here. I wondered whether I would have faced the abuse that I had. Oh, how different my life could have been.

I then opened one of the books. It was Mum's personal diary. It had entries of dates before I was born. I remember reading entries from 1986. She talked about her sin and being thankful for the gift that God had given her a little girl. Though she had fallen and done something she shouldn't have, she was grateful that she had me. That was my first little confirmation that my dad was not my dad. My stepbrothers were right. A part of me was glad they were right because that way it justified their actions. It also was a way for my brain to understand why I could be abused and Dad act like he did not care. I wasn't his, so why would I matter that much?

I fell asleep after reading these entries, and that day the dreams started; I now recognise them as memories instead of just mere dreams. My mind went back to when Mum was still around. She used to ask me to call Dad by his given name. And when I did call him Dad, he would respond. I can still hear my mum's voice saying to call him by his name. When she was gone I kept calling him that but then would feel very awkward because everybody else, including Mum's son, Ethan, called him Dad. I decided I would too.

The first time I called him Dad, he ignored me, and I was really hurt. It was really awkward to call him Dad and for him to ignore. After a few days, though, it became second nature and he responded to Dad. Now that I am older I can understand why he reacted as he did. Sometimes only age can put things in perspective.

The next day I was back in the box and found another treasure. There in a book, side by side, lay my and my brother's birth certificate. I looked at mine and realised the second name on it was not my actual given name. The name that means 'Purity' in my mother's tongue was written in big, bold letters. I stared at it for a while. I went by the name 'Patience' with Dad's name as my surname. On the certificate only my first and second names appeared. Patience was my grandma's middle name. I realised that Mum probably called me that as a pet name and everybody assumed it was my name and so it stuck. As she was not around to correct us, Patience became my official name.

My name had been changed from a name which meant 'pure or clean' to one which meant 'to wait' or 'patient'. From Purity to being Patience, God was truly in the details as my life came to reflect. I have needed so much patience in my life and cannot really say it has been a very pure and clean life. God gave me what I needed after Mum passed away, patience. As I write this book he is restoring my name, Purity, as he is cleansing me and making me clean and pure once again.

On my birth certificate Mum's name was on the mother's name slot and a string of X's was on the father's spot. I quickly looked at my brother's certificate. On his birth certificate his father's name was clearly written and he had a surname too. His dad was the man I had come to call dad too. Right there in my hands was the smoking gun and the second very clear evidence that truly my dad was not my biological father. God was clearly giving me answers.

If I knew any of this when I was still a hopeless soul, I would have ended it all. But at this stage of my life God was teaching me to lean on him, to trust in him, to be patient, and not to lean on my own understanding. The tapestry of my life was coming alive. He was showing me that things are never what they seem and was teaching me to always take a step back and look at the bigger picture. The bigger picture, in this case, showed me that he had provided me with a father, not a perfect one, but who was willing enough to bring me up and not to separate me from my brother. Not many men willingly look after a child that's not theirs biologically or who is not related at all in the absence of the child's biological mother. My dad did. And for that I am forever grateful.

The question of where Mum is spending eternity always bothered me. I kept asking God for a sign, any sign that Mum was okay and was with him. I took the diary I had found and kept reading. She had written a lot of articles about God and the Bible. I kept reading, smiling to myself, as I realised just how similar she and I were. I wrote too, I sang as she did, and I had been described as having a soft soprano voice. These same words I saw she had written to describe her singing voice. She sang in the church where she worshipped. WThen I got to the middle of the book there were a few pages whose edges had been glued together. I slowly pried them opened. She had written her testimony, dated 1984.

She wrote how as a pastor's kid she had thought she was safe and that her father's salvation would cover her. She had grown up in church often serving and doing good things; therefore there was no reason for her to make a decision to accept salvation for herself. In short, she was a good person. It was not until a pastor at an open air crusade preached and explained that each and every person is answerable to God, that we were all sinners who have fallen short of God's glory, that she realised neither her good deeds nor her pastor father would get her to heaven. She had to make the decision for herself. And she did. Oh, the joy that flowed in my soul at that moment. There it was, the sign I had asked for so many times. God is indeed faithful.

My maternal grandfather, Ron, was a pastor and was married to Esther, a very humble and patient woman. As I was learning more about Mum I started learning even more about the things that happened in the years since Mum passed away. Dad had a few files he kept in a locked cupboard. He never allowed anyone to touch them but, for some reason, he trusted me to get different things from this file. Dad has a peculiar habit of filing every letter he received and when he wrote one he filed a copy of what he wrote. Of course I was going to be a curious little thing and read some of them.

I saw letters from my maternal grandpa to Dad, and vice versa, and they concerned me. I read them. My grandfather had requested to take my brother and me. He was willing to look after me but was adamant that I was not to be separated from my brother. He called us his children. Dad refused in his reply and said he was going to look after us himself. He did agree that we should not be separated.

Other letters were between dad and his ex-wife, Elisa. She was not a happy camper! These letters were accusatory, saying things like Dad should send me and his new wife away as all we did was eat and use up resources that should be for her children. The letters were so full of vile and hate. I couldn't believe I was reading half of them. The words she used were the same things I heard my stepbrothers, her sons, tell me over and over again. I realised they were getting these words from her. They were piercing words.

Dad's reply was surprising. He always defended me and his new wife. He fought for me not only to his ex-wife but over the years to anybody who tried to say anything against me or any of his family. I admire him for that. If he taught us one thing, he taught us to be principled and to always stand by our word. He also told me over and over again to always stand by my choices, and to make them very carefully so as to never say, 'I wish I knew!' Regret was and is not in his dictionary and he taught us never to use that phrase by making sure we never did anything that would lead to regret down the line. He truly is a man to be admired in many ways.

CHAPTER FIFTEEN

I have long learned that I can't blame God. I can blame man. Many people over the years have asked me why I don't blame God. After all, he is all knowing. Why didn't God stop it? Why did John have to be born if God knew he was going to do such a terrible thing? Why was Hitler born? Why are there starving children? If God was to stop all these people and events then none of us would be alive today. Why you ask? Because we all, in our own little way, make mistakes that affect another negatively. To us it might be a little small incident but to the victim it might be the worst thing anyone had ever done to them. So suppose God stopped all things men chose to do and this person prayed that you would not exist to do the wrong you did to them. Would you be alive? And what would that make God? A creator of free will people or a puppet master?

We measure right or wrong using our own skewed measure and this changes from person to person and region to region. We do not have a set standard for it., We also change this standard. For example, we keep crying about what Hitler did or the genocide in Rwanda or the terrorist attacks and yet we kill children in the womb in the name of pro–choice. Who is speaking for the millions of unborn children being aborted every day? If God was to stop this evil by eliminating all responsible, how many of us will be innocent? I know I am not even though I have never done it myself. I, for one, am thankful for God's mercy and grace because if I am punished as I deserve, I will not be alive. I am also thankful that God is a just God, and all things that seem unfair now will receive just judgement from he who is a righteous judge. He has the right standard of good and evil, the right standard of right and wrong. His position never changes and is the same today, yesterday, and forever. May my standard be found in him.

When you throw a rock in still waters, the ripple goes further than the point of entry of the rock. In the same way, you might think that stealing one little thing will not affect anyone else, but that ripple affects more than just the immediate people around us. Just because you haven't killed millions does not mean you haven't killed one. God cares for the one as much as he cares for the millions. We lie, we steal, we call others names, we put others down, we are jealous, and we malign others' name. Every one of those actions affects someone else negatively and that ripple travels a far distance. Then, in turn, in the name of getting even or learning a lesson they go and do the same to another, and that action affects many others. So your one action affects hundreds or thousands and sometimes millions! You have heard it said that man is not an island. In the same way no individual action and decision only affect the primary person (as much as we lie to ourselves it doesn't affect others.) And the cycle goes on. Many would not like to admit it but the truth of the matter is hurt people hurt others.

Not to be simplistic but there are starving children in the world because someone somewhere has decided to be greedy enough to enrich themselves and not help another. They are there because some people have made an unfair world economic system that's only concerned about self and no one else. There's war because of the same issue—self. We are so concerned about our selfishness and self-worship that it consumes us. Then we turn round and ask if there's a righteous God or if there's a God at all. Have we looked at ourselves? In the beginning, God created a perfect world able to cater for all and it was good. Then he entrusted us (humans) to maintain it and look after it, but instead we have continually destroyed it, destroyed ourselves in the process. We then boldly turn around and blame God and even question his existence. Psalm 14:1(NIV) says that the fool says in his heart, 'There is no God.' Again our selfishness and self-love has to blame another instead of acknowledging we are the ones in the wrong and asking the creator to help us set it right again. We do not take responsibility of our actions. Blaming God is giving us more licences to destroy it even more. After all, we can always say he is responsible!

We ask God to stop these people and these unfair things happening in our world, yet we are not willing to give up our 'freedoms'! We can't have our cake and eat it too. It is either we have the free will to love or to hate, to serve or to demand service, to hurt or to nurture, or we are robots in God's hands. If God stops every bad thing that our hearts decide to do, then he created robots. Therefore, he would be a liar because he created us to have that free will. We would then turn around and ask why God is forcing us to do things his way, forcing us to love him. Clearly, we humans are never satisfied. I have heard it said that *'Freedom is not the right to do what we want, but the right to do what we ought!'* (Jim Caviezel's interview with Dave Cooper on YouTube.) God gives us instructions on how to use our free will and do what we ought; love the Lord our God and love our neighbours as ourselves. If we do this then and only then can we say we are free.

John chose to do what he did, Dad chose to react as he did, my stepbrothers chose to do what they did, and so did my childhood friends. At the end of the day they each had the freedom to do what they chose. They used it to do what they wanted and not what they ought to. At the end of the day I also had to choose and still have to choose what and how I react to it all. Will I let those experiences make me bitter or better? Will I let those experiences influence how I interact with others?

For example, every John I have met I have been wary of. John, a Hebrew name that means 'God has been gracious, has shown favour' had been turned into a negative in my mind. John did not show any grace or mercy in his dealings with me. He did the very opposite. It almost became a daily prayer that I will never be associated with a John or God forbid my husband be a John, as the name reminded me of my assaulter. A man by the same name had a crush on me through university. There was no attraction on my side but he had the added disadvantage of his name. By the end of the four years he was so heartbroken. One day he told me that because the love of his life—me—wanted nothing to do with him he would never get married. I felt sorry for him every time he asked me why I did not give him a chance. I often wonder where he is and hope he quickly got over me.

I take this opportunity to apologise to the Johns I have met over the years, especially if I treated you poorly. Unfortunately, most of you were paying for the sins of another before you. God has a sense of humour though. I have met so many Johns and every variation of the name when I came to Australia, and they are the some of the best guys I have ever met. It is as though God is trying to remind me that a part of the population should not pay for the sins of one man.

Meanwhile, the hours I spent alone were spent with God, reading, dancing by myself, listening, and learning more about God and who he was. My faith grew in my loneliness. I think this is when I started to see people for who they really were, broken people who reacted according to their environment, and lived according to what life had dished to them. I realised that we all make choices every day, whether we realise it or not. We make a choice to live with our pain or despite our pain. We make a choice to love or hate. We make a choice to forgive or become bitter with unforgiveness. We make a choice knowingly or unknowingly to let God heal us or remain wounded. I also realised, looking around me, that not making a choice or not thinking about it is also a choice, and this choice is the worst of them all. Those on the fence always fall on the wrong side of the fence.

This was my season of choices. I had to choose how I perceived the world around me and the people in it. God slowly started to show me the heart of people around me and through that taught me to be more sympathetic to people. Don't get me wrong, I do not like what happened to me whether through John, Dad not protecting me, my stepbrothers, or my friends. But I can confidently tell you that when I think of any of these people I don't think of them with hate or anger. I think of them with sympathy and forgiveness. I think of them as broken people hurting others. I often wonder what triggered their reactions and actions in life. I also realise that if I let that stuff determine how I react and view life I will turn into them, and I will, in turn, affect others in my life and world. I choose forgiveness. I choose life!

Forgiveness is another hard topic for most and truthfully one of the hardest things to do. I reached a point and realised that the lives of those who hurt me were going on and seemed to be going great. I was drinking the poison of unforgiveness and expecting them to die. Many of them will be quite shocked at what's contained in this book because they forgot about it. The hurt people are the ones who carry the pain. The perpetrators rarely remember what they did. That burden was too heavy so I chose to forgive. I realised quite early that just saying I forgive you is not enough. Sometimes, even after saying those words, one will sit down and think of the people that hurt you with anger and bitterness.

I went through this many times. I realised that forgiveness, without the author of it, is near impossible. I prayed and asked God to give me his forgiveness, to help me forgive. God has given the biggest sacrifice in history—he forgives us. He teaches us to pray for forgiveness as we forgive others. It is not until you need forgiveness that you understand the importance of forgiving others. I know I need forgiveness from God for my bad choices, and in turn, God expects me to forgive those who hurt me. He has taught me to forgive and consequently I have a more peaceful life.

Does that mean they are off the hook? Not at all. God is a God of justice! Just because those who do bad things seem to be living a prosperous life does not mean that God has forgotten your tears. He collects your tears and stores them in a bottle, every last drop of it (Psalm 56:8 NIV). And he also says that man has been appointed to live once and then comes judgement (Hebrews 9:27 NIV). Those tears will be answered for, every last drop of it. God is not man that he should lie or change his mind (Numbers 23:19 NIV). God, who has every right to punish us all for all the evil we do, is patient with us and readily forgives us (Romans 9:22 NIV; Nehemiah 9:17b NIV).

I pray that they too will make their peace with God and seek God's forgiveness because I wouldn't wish God's wrath and judgment on even my worst enemy. God knows how he will punish them he is the judge. I have no right to be a judge for their actions because by condemning them, I condemn myself. I am not righteous myself. I'm a sinner as they are. I am as human as they are. That puts things into perspective for me and it humbles me to let God be the judge as I guard my salvation with fear and trembling. At the end of the day my actions and choices will be laid bare before God and he will not allow me to use another as an excuse for my choices or way of life. That will be on me and I'll have to answer for myself, they for their lives, and you for yours. Choose today which side of that judgement you want to be on. The side of the redeemed or on the side of the judged. Choose today whom you will serve.

CHAPTER SIXTEEN

In years seven and eight at school I had a great friend called Winnie. We had been in the same class but different stream right from year three. We were never close but when things blew up with my neighbour's best friend we grew closer. She was a boarding student. She was the total opposite of me. She was tall and slim with the most beautiful dark skin. I was short, round, and had what some friends called the yellow skin. She was also a Catholic, while I was a Born Again Christian. She came from a rich family with her dad working for the UN and she had been to a few countries around the world, while I had never even been to the airport nor even seen any of our country's borders.

She had everything I didn't and yet she was the most humble person I had known. She treated me as an equal and trusted me with her life and her stories. I remember when she was going through her confirmation. She came to me with a list of names and asked me what new name I would pick for her. We joked about it with me picking the worst names on the list. They were all names that started with *C*, for a reason I can't remember right now, and the name Clarice comes to mind. I don't know whether that was one of the names I had suggested or whether that's the name we decided to go with.

I looked forward to school and break times just so I could spend time with my dear friend. Little did I know just what a big part she would play in my life for the next six years. We had the best time and I remember her with such great memories.

We did our national exams in year eight and in my heart I was really sad as I knew I would not see dear Winnie again. On the closing day, she invited me to go stay with her and her family for a week. I was excited, but I wasn't sure Dad would share my enthusiasm. But he surprised me by letting me go. Oh, how I was excited! Dad had never let us go to any sleepover, let alone visit for a week! I think he knew I would be miserable staying in the compound with no one to talk to and nothing to do.

We had the best time that week and at the end of the week I was sad again. Winnie suggested I call Dad and ask if I could stay another week. He agreed. I couldn't believe it! And so our time together continued. During that time we shared a lot. We read in silence sometimes, watched movies, cleaned, and talked about God and the Bible. To me it was like a kid in a candy store! They had a fridge and could eat anything from it, had movies, a big house. Winnie and I stayed in an all-girls bedroom and for the first time in my life I was sleeping in the same room with a girl. That was the best sleepover I have ever had. I was resting, I was at peace, and I was healing.

Time came to go home though and after the Christmas holiday it was time to join a high school. She went to a private co-ed day high school in Nairobi while I went to a national girls' public high school. We kept in touch during those years, often writing letters as long as eleven A4 papers, both sides written. We talked about school, life in high school, boys, but most importantly we encouraged each other in faith and God. The letters kept going back and forth. She was the only person I ever wrote a letter to throughout high school, apart from the one letter I wrote to my Dad to tell him I had arrived safely at school at the beginning of each term. Those letters became famous in my dorm. Whenever the prefect got the letters and saw a fat envelope, she would call me even without looking at the name. They always wondered what and who took the time to write such long letters. Of course for the longest time most thought it was a boy and nothing would convince them otherwise.

Unfortunately, we lost touch after high school and met once a few years later. I was amazed at the lady I met. She was Born Again, was doing ministry at her church, wanted to learn Japanese so she could teach English in Japan, and she was glowing, so full of joy. She remembered those letters too and we talked a while about those days. She, I'm sure, appreciates those years and the support we gave each other in those very hard years called the teens.

I loved high school. It was my escape from home. I looked forward to the day I would board the bus and travel six hours to school. When I got there I would get my writing pad, pen a letter to dad to let him know I had arrived safely and bury myself in school work and school activities. I was a member of the school choir, the St John's ambulance club, ranger's club, voluntary club, and Red Cross. Any club that was set up to help people I was a member.

We had visiting days one Saturday a month during the term. We had twelve to sixteen weeks in a term. On visiting days family and friends were allowed to come and spend the day with the students. They would bring along home cooked food for a picnic and any essentials that the student would need at school. Every student looked forward to this day so much so that on the day there would be students standing at the gate waiting for their parents. I was never there. I used visiting days to catch up with chores, sleep, sit in the field on my own, or practise my piano playing. Not that I wasn't visited but if I wasn't, it never made a difference to me.

Many times someone would come visiting me and several hours would be spent looking for me. My parents, or whoever came to visit, would get so annoyed. Thinking back it was unfair on them. Well, I knew we were not well off and sometimes Dad would struggle to pay my fees. I was also not the only one in high school. My elder brothers were too. In my head the letter their mum wrote about me using up what was theirs kept ringing and that was enough to make me want to be independent.

I remember telling my dad to give me less pocket money than the KSH1200 (AUD18) he was giving me a month. In my head, I thought it was unfair that I was being given so much while my brothers were probably getting nothing or very little. I asked for KSH300 (AUD 5). My brothers were shocked that I would do that when I told them about it years later. They thought I should have taken it and given them some of it. Was 300 enough? Far from it! But I survived. The school served all meals, three square meals, and served tea for morning tea and afternoon tea, so I wasn't going to starve. I also did a big shop at the beginning of the term for essentials and if I ran out whoever came to visit would bring some along. Pocket money was just for snacks and other wants, not needs. This is where friends like B2 were great. They shared what they had, no questions asked. We called her B2 and we still do (I didn't know about bananas in pyjamas until I came to Australia, so no relation to that B2).

I remember B2 sharing her bread at teatime or buying an avocado and sharing it with me at dinner time. We were not even in the same dining hall, let alone dorm, but she shared with me. She made me at ease and never made me feel like I had nothing. I had several other friends who did the same. Some gave me their uniforms when they were done with school; therefore, I never needed to buy any more uniforms through school. B2 stands out from them all for her generous heart and her loud infectious laugh. She made me enjoy high school and do it with a big smile on my face. She was also my partner in crime and we often got into much mischief.

Speaking of mischief in high school, one day in year twelve a classmate told me of a teacher's house we could have our hair straightened at. In high school, we were not allowed to chemically straighten our hair and we were not allowed to have it plaited either. We also were not allowed to have blow dryers so it was a constant struggle to brush it every morning. I had my air chemically straightened throughout primary school and so had to shave it off in high school. I had short hair all through high school. I was sad to see my long hair gone. When I heard we had a teacher straightening hair at his house for a small fee, we were excited. Part of me knew it was wrong, but the excitement of having my hair more manageable was too big a temptation. A group of us went, paid the fee, and had our hair blow-dried.

Well, the days and weeks went by until one Saturday a list of the girls who went was released. The girl had been caught and had been told to write the name of everyone who had ever gone there. I was one of them.

On Monday morning we were all called to the principal's office after a tongue lashing at the school assembly that morning. I had never been in the principal's office. We called it the *red carpo* (red carpet) because the whole office floor had a red carpet. I couldn't believe that I had been good all through high school and now, in the last year, I had messed up with just a few weeks to go! I feared we would get a suspension and if we did I would be in hot water with Dad. I was not looking forward to that conversation.

The advantage of the whole situation is that it was a big group and it included high ranking prefects and teachers' children. All we could hope for is a lenient punishment. We were very remorseful and admitted it was a very silly thing to do. She called us all manner of names, 'golden disgusting girls' comes to mind. Golden because we were the candidate class of the golden jubilee of the school, disgusting because of what we had done. After a while of listening to her talk she handed a pair of scissors to us and asked us to go out to the middle of the field far away from everyone else and shave each other's hair. We expected a harsher sentence but it never came. The disappointment in my music teacher, who was also the chaplain, was punishment enough, and in a class of eight music students there was nowhere to hide. That's why my hair was even shorter hair in my last year of high school.

Another friends that made an impact in high school was Cara. She was my best friend. She had deep thoughts and was very intelligent. She was also studying music like I was and we spent a lot of time together. One of the most memorable days with Cara was when as a school choir, we were given a standing ovation singing the 'Hallelujah' chorus in the National Music Festival in Nairobi. That was our best performance ever! Cara sang the alto and when we hit that last note with people raising to their feet, she collapsed. I remember the panic in me but also the rush of adrenaline as a first aider. She was rushed to the hospital. She had a migraine. Thankfully her mum was also around on that day. We won that competition. Cara and I wrote poetry and songs and served in the Christian Union Intercessory group together.

Di and Kari encouraged me a lot in my faith. The latter left school to relocate to the US after year nine so I only knew her for a year. The impact of that short time together still remains. Di and I, though, kept going. We prayed and fasted for days on end at break time in the chapel. Sometimes B2 joined us. Di also wrote songs and we spent hours singing together.

I never dated in high school. Not because of a lack of suitors but because in my head and heart I knew it was a waste of time. I had decided that if and when I got into a relationship it would be for the long term. I wasn't going to have casual relationships or anything like that. Being in an all-girls school we would crave male in our midst and I watched in amusement as girls threw themselves at the few men around; the grounds men, the young single teachers, the sons of the teachers who lived in the compound and the nurse's son. These men seemed to be the most handsome men around purely because they were the constant testosterone in the compound. We also had open days and symposiums when other schools would come and of course these schools had boys too. Again I would be amused watching the tactics of my colleagues on these days. B2 and I loved watching these girls and reading the letters that would follow these rendezvous. Nobody ever used their true names and when we had these schools over we would not allow our friends to call us by our real names, lest we receive the said letters.

B2 and I and a few other people in our class made it our business to grade the letters written by boys to girls in our class. The receiver would read it and pass it around the class and we would mark the grammar and flow of the letter, as though marking a composition complete with comments. These letters would sometimes be sent back to sender. We loved doing that. Most of these boys and girls were not being serious. They were looking to hook up with one or another for bragging rights, and I hated it. They would have several girlfriends and several boyfriends in different schools across the country and perhaps a few more at home on holidays. I wasn't going to fall for that.

I spent hours writing novels, songs and poetry in high school. I even wrote a few plays. Writing and creating characters had become my escape. It was great to create these characters and stories. I loved living their lives and stories. I wrote a lot of short stories and these stories became longer and longer. I had started writing a novel in year nine, and I used to have my dorm mates standing by ready to read the next page. And then would wait for me to finish the next and on and on. They loved the stories I wrote and kept encouraging me to keep going. I was given a lot of suggestions on where the story should go. I finished writing the novel in year twelve and started the sequel a year later. Unfortunately my step-mum burnt all my paperwork, which included my sequel novel, some poetry, some short story, all of my mum's memorabilia, and a lot things I had collected over the years. They were destroyed because they were water damaged after a flood in the house. My one regret was leaving them at Dad's house. My heart was broken and I have never fully recovered from it. What a loss.

High school did pass by quickly enough, though I missed aspects of it as we all sometimes do. I wasn't brilliant academically but looking back I realise I would have performed much better if I showed much more interest in it. I am one of those people who applies themselves 100 per cent in topics and things of interest and only 10 per cent on other things. I wrote poems in chemistry class, composed songs in physics class, dozed in computer class, hated biology, and daydreamed in maths class. I just didn't understand a whole lot in these classes and was placed in remedial maths in year twelve. We had a great teacher maths, and he made it fun! For the first time in high school I enjoyed maths and looked forward to maths. I understood it but to my dismay it was too little too late. I had always believed I was bad at maths but my remedial teacher proved to me that I wasn't. I just hadn't understood the teaching style of my previous teacher, and that had determined my attitude for the rest of my high school career. As for the other sciences, I actually loved physics more than I did the other two, with chemistry being the worst. I couldn't wait to be done with them.

I was quite excited to be in English, Christian Religious Education, Kiswahili, and my personal favourite, Music. My national year twelve results reflect this of course. My strength was in the practical subjects—the arts. I didn't fail in my exams but I didn't score enough to be called into university for medicine or engineering. I was happy with my results. I had scored enough to join university and I would be able to concentrate on my strength—the arts. I couldn't study music though because according to Dad it doesn't pay! I could do that after first degree he said, so I did the second best thing: sociology. I somehow found myself in university studying a Bachelor of Science in Disaster Management and International Diplomacy.

CHAPTER SEVENTEEN

When I was in high school my grandma fell sick. She started asking my dad to take us to see her. I was in year twelve. That meant shorter holidays and more school work because of the upcoming national exams. In one such school holiday my dad decided to take us. Grandma had requested that my step-mum, Dana, be brought along, as she wanted to see her and know who was looking after her children—namely, my brother and I. We all went.

We didn't have much to do with my grandparents after Mum died. We had only been there a couple of times before this time. I had always wanted to go and missed that side of my family but Dad preferred us going to his home during holidays. A part of me felt like he was denying me a chance to know who I am but I had no say in the matter, so I never said a thing. I have come to learn over the years that Grandma and Grandpa always remembered us.

They would send my aunties and cousins to visit us and ask how we were doing. Even before I knew that my dad was not my father I had always wondered why they would ask my brother and I how our new mother treated us. Then, when no one else was around, they would ask me how Dad treated me. It turned out that Grandpa was keeping an eye and ear out for me. I always said all was well, so none of them knew about the things that happened in the dead of night when I was seven. I didn't open up to anyone until I was an adult. Now I wish I had opened up earlier but at the same time realise that my upbringing would have been very different and I would probably not be where I am today.

When we got there my brother and I left the grown-ups talking. Well, it was more like an interview in my eyes, as they asked my mum lots of questions. We had better things to do, like run around Grandpa's compound and catch up with cousins and aunties who were around. At some point I turned a corner and came face to face with my grandpa Ron. I will never forget that conversation. It was also the last conversation I ever had with him.

'Your dad tells me you sing and that you wrote a song for the national competitions?' he asked, referring to the child labour song my fellow music students and I wrote in year eleven.

'Yes,' I said. 'I enjoy singing and music.'

'Your mum, Sarah, loved singing too,' he said with a smile. 'She had a soft soprano just like you. She would be so proud of you.'

I felt great. I was happy and proud that he saw her in me and that I was making her proud. And then he said something else that surprised me. 'Your dad also tells me you are now Born Again, and you love God.'

I was really surprised by this. I was still hiding my Christianity, or so I thought. I never said anything to my dad, or any of my family for that matter. It was not a topic we were allowed to speak on. Yet here was my grandfather, proudly looking at me and telling me that my dad told him about my salvation. I confirmed the story to him. He looked at me proudly and encouraged me to keep at it and then he turned and walked back into the house where Dad, Mum, and Grandma were still talking.

We had lunch together amidst much laughter and joy. My grandparents promised my step-mum that next time she came they would slaughter a goat for her—the highest honour to a guest in mum's culture. We went back home not realising that was the last time I would see Grandma alive and that new week would be her last week.

The following week I was back in school for tuition school. That Saturday was going to be Aunt Hannah's church wedding. I was going to miss that. Everybody in my maternal extended family was present for the wedding, but I wasn't.

Grandma was struggling that day with her diabetes. Her blood sugar was low. She asked for Fanta to boost her sugar and collapsed a short while later. Her sons carried her to a car, left the wedding, and tried to rush her to hospital. Hospitals there are not five minutes away and there were rough roads. They were up country after all. The story they tell is that Grandma came to at some point, looked around, and then in her language, Kamba, she said, 'Thank you, God, for letting me see all my children.' She smiled and breathed her last. She was still smiling.

That same week I was taken out of school to attend her funeral. It wasn't a sad funeral, not for me anyway. And though we all knew we would miss her, we all knew she was at rest and safe in the arms of Jesus. Grandpa was heartbroken though, his love was gone. Viewing her body was like looking at someone asleep. She was so beautiful and peaceful. She still had that smile on her face. I remember thinking that if I lived my life serving God, even if doing just half what this woman had done in hers, I would be doing great. I didn't know much about Grandma but the little I did know demanded respect. And not forced respect. She was a gentle, loving, patient matriarch. She was the ideal pastor's wife. She and Grandpa worked like a well-oiled machine. They were interdependent, yet independent. The little I saw of their marriage actually gave me hope for my own.

She was buried and life went on. That was in 2004. Two years later, word came that Grandpa wanted to see my brother and I. Dad couldn't afford the fare needed and he couldn't afford the time off from work either. Three of us were just about to join university and that was going to be one expensive venture.

Grandpa was so sick that his children brought him to The city for treatment late in 2006. That's when we got a chance to see him. We arrived at my aunt's house where he was and spent half a day there. He couldn't speak. He just looked at me. Those eyes still haunt me. He looked like he wanted to say something but couldn't say anything. He couldn't stand or walk either, so my cousin carried him everywhere, bathed him, changed him and saw to his every need. It was decided he needed to go to the hospital immediately. On that day he was admitted in hospital.

Ron was born in 1922. He was the first born of Noah and Eva. He joined the army in 1941, Second World War East African Armed Service Corps, as a driver (I had not even known he had been in the army until the visit when I had the last conversation with him. He told me a little about his army days in Egypt as we had lunch).

He served in various places, including Egypt, for several years. He also worked in a sisal factory. He and Esther had eleven children. In 1952, together with his wife, they came to know the Lord and joined catechism. They were baptised in 1954. He became a church elder and was posted to an AIC Church as a pastor. He served in at least six churches and was gifted in church planting, motivating his congregants in putting up churches. He was an inspiring preacher and he won many souls for the Lord. He retired in December 2005 after decades of dedicated service. He was also the chairman of various primary schools and served in many other development projects. He was a man of the people. He loved development and offered his time and resources to uplift the welfare of the community.

He passed away on Sunday, the twenty-sixth of November 2006. He was survived by nine children at the time, two of whom have since passed on, thirty-six grandchildren, and many greatgrandchildren. Once again, we were at his home in viewing his body and finally buried him. He was buried next to his wife, who was buried next to their daughter, Sarah, my mother. Just like his wife he looked peaceful and happy. I kept wondering when he would wake up because he looked like he was sleeping. He died of a broken heart, I think. He couldn't live without his love. He had prostate cancer and decided he would not tell anyone about it because he just wanted to go home to God and to be with his love.

His was a life well-lived. I had no idea about what he had done or achieved in his life until the day of his funeral and his eulogy was read. I had always just thought him as a simple man, a pastor. I realised just how little I had known about him and his experiences, his service to God, his passions, and his life. The more I heard of him, the more I was proud to be his granddaughter. He had done much and achieved even more as simple and humble as he had been.

CHAPTER EIGHTEEN

Gap year was an interesting year. I was home again for an undetermined period of time. I wasn't looking forward to it. Immediately after I finished high school, I asked to go visit with my friend and classmate, Rehema's, family. And just like four years before, Dad agreed. So off I went and spent the rest of 2004 with them. I had the time of my life, met most of her relatives and extended family, had Christmas with them, and then even visited an aunty and stayed a while in a different part of town. I enjoyed it a lot.

Rehema and I were music students in a class of eight and classmates. Our music teacher was pressing us to write a school anthem, as the one we had was written by the British during colonial times and talked of Jacarandas and Nandi Flames. It was really boring! The eight of us saw it as a daunting task and for two years, between year eleven and twelve, she kept asking us to write one. In year eleven, the eight of us wrote a song on child labour that went all the way into the national competitions and we came third. The first two were written by professionals, so to us that was a tremendous achievement. I conducted that choir. I loved conducting.

I remember very well how nervous I was in that amphitheatre in the KICC building, feeling all eyes were on me and knowing that I would have to introduce and conduct the choir. I was so nervous that when the bell rang to start I forgot to pick up the microphone to speak into it but instead just spoke. The singing went well but we lost marks because the song was in English and Swahili. They expected the song to be in one language. We were elated though for coming third.

Anyway, our teacher was convinced that we could write the school song, so she kept asking us to. Finally, in year twelve, Rehema and I decided to put pen to paper. She was great at poetry and I had composed a few tunes on the piano. She showed me one of her poems that she thought would be appropriate for a school song and together we put the two together. One day, I was in the chapel playing the song when out of nowhere my teacher showed up, and of course asks me what it is I was playing. I explained that Rehema and I were working on the school song. She asked us to sing it in music class, and the eight of us started working on it. Weeks later we introduced it to the school. A few short months later we finished our exams and we were gone. I have since learned that the school still uses our song as the school anthem and that another music student, two years behind us, harmonised it and it sounds great. I had an opportunity to hear it once at a music festival and I was so proud and excited as to how far it had come.

Rehema and I have kept in touch over the years. When she is in Nairobi she has sometimes stayed with my parents. We are still friends and I can honestly say when I count my friends, she is definitely one of them.

CHAPTER NINETEEN

I was free of school in 2005 and had a long year ahead of me. I decided this was the time to start going to church again. At this time Mum and Dad had also started to go to church. I joined their church. Soon, I was playing the keyboard at church and became great friends with one of the senior pastor's daughter and shortly became a friend with the rest of the family.

The biggest lesson I learned from this church was taught by the pastor's wife. She said the simplest thing but in my head it is as though a light bulb went on. She encouraged us that if we wanted to get married in the future we'd best start praying for our husbands and wives as soon as now. I took that seriously and I started praying. I had seen less than ideal marriages around me. Deep down I detested men because of what was done to me and the reaction of the men around me. Perhaps that was the reason I didn't want to date and maybe that's the reason I made a lot of male friends. It was a case of keep your friends close and your enemies closer! But I knew I wanted to get married and that God had to change me, heal me, and bring along the right man. It became part of my regular prayer.

One day I decided to venture out on my own and decided to go to a different church. There was nothing wrong with Dad's church but I felt I was going there just because they did. I needed to find my own place and my own home. I went to a youth church across town, and I fell in love with it right there and then. It became my home and I still consider it my home church.

I started serving there. I sang in the youth choir, was part of the seeker's team (the drama team), helped with cleaning of the church in the middle of the week with a group called the *Ex-cans* (short for ex-candidates who were ex high school kids on their gap year), attended the school holiday three-day seminars, made a lot of friends, and together we did a lot of ministry work in our area. We did door to door ministry, collected clothes, sorted them and distributed them with a friend who had started a clothes bank. As usual, I found myself surrounded by men. I remember, more than once, turning up for these ministries and there would be ten or twelve of us and I would be the only girl. Sometimes there would be only one other. They became my brothers and they looked after me like I was their little sister. I really enjoyed doing ministry with them.

One of my fondest memories of that time was a day I met Pastor Nathan, our youth pastor, in the corridors on one weekday afternoon and he called me by all my three names. I almost cried. The youth church had about 700 young people in it. I never thought anyone would know my second name, let alone my surname! He did. He knew my name in full! That was the first time in my life I felt like I was part of something, that I was fully accepted and someone actually cared about me. I was so touched by that single event. I belonged.

My dad was shocked every time he saw me hugging one of the young men I was doing ministry with from church. I was getting increasingly frustrated because he clearly did not know me. His idea of 'the talk' was, 'You go ahead and get pregnant or get AIDS. That will be your problem!'

Oh, he put the fear of God in me with that talk. One day I was walking home and I met a young man that I knew was a drunk and a smoker. He lived two blocks from our house. He was telling me all about his music and decided that he was a gentleman so would like to make sure I got home safely. He took me right to my front door. Mum was not impressed and couldn't wait to tell Dad. Well, there was fire and brimstone in the house that night, and nothing I said would convince them that I had nothing to do with the guy.

For the next few weeks Dad would come home and scream his lungs out about me not listening, dressing inappropriately and still seeing this good for nothing boy. I had no idea what he was talking about. He said

I was wearing really short skirts and make-up, two things that I did not like nor own.

I finally learned that there was a girl about my height and skin colour who lived in our estate. She was dating this man! I was so angry and that day I told Dad off. I couldn't believe he couldn't verify his story and he couldn't believe me when I told him I had nothing to do with the boy. It turns out Dad was friends with the boy's watchman. The watchman kept reporting that he had been seeing me coming into the house to visit this boy. He had only seen me once, so he didn't really know me, and because this girl lived in the same place he concluded it was me.

That I can understand, but my dad taking his word above mine I couldn't. He never believed what I said and he proved that over and over again in my life. I waited for an apology or acknowledgement that he was wrong but that never has and never will come. My dad never apologises. As he taught us, never regret anything. I think he takes that lesson too literally. He never admits when he is wrong.

One of the three-day seminars that my youth pastor held was titled 'Eyes that See'. Pastor Nathan was teaching us to write down what our goals in life were and to put these goals in their category. We were to write about our careers, our ideal partners, our children, how we would like to raise our children. Anything we thought we wanted in our future we were to prayerfully write it down and then spend a few minutes every week reading them and praying over them. Once again I took this assignment seriously and I wrote. I had already started praying for my husband. That part was easy to write down as I had thought about it for many hours and many days.

Fast forward to years later when I got engaged to Zane and I was surprised just how much of what I prayed for he was. I described him exactly, even his character. He is my answer to prayer and truly a dream come true.

There was an international mission happening in Nairobi, and the Nairobi congregations were looking for volunteers to help the international short-term missionaries. The mission was being led African mission and brought together people from USA, Canada, UK, New Zealand, Australia, Zimbabwe, South Africa, Uganda, Kenya and many other African countries. My friend, Sophie, from church and I signed up. Little did I know that was the start of one of the greatest adventures of my life, with plenty of laughs, tears, and God always showing up on time.

Sophie is a great friend. A lot of people thought we were sisters. We were always laughing and doing something fun together. After the month of volunteering as local missionaries we decided to sign up for a year of youth missionary work called the African Youth Mission that ran through African Mission. We also decided to volunteer at a children's home in the area. Dad did not allow me to do either and Sophie ended up doing both. I was sad and disappointed.

When I look back at the friends I have had over the years, Sophie is one of the most precious friends I have ever had. I thank God for her and for the opportunity to meet her and to know her. We have had great times together and not so great times together, but through it all we still remain friends. She is one of those friends that no matter how long we take without speaking to each other we will pick up where we left off. I value that friendship, and I know sometimes I did take it for granted. I regret those moments. Regardless, I count her as one of my dearest friends. She is one of the most generous, positive and fun people I know. She likes people for them and doesn't try to change who they are. She celebrates each person as they are and makes them feel confident in themselves.

I didn't have a passport and certainly had no money to get one. Sophie paid for me to get one as we needed a passport to be in the African Youth Mission team. I'll never forget the day she called me to get our photos taken. I was having a majorly bad hair day and I didn't even have fare to get there. She didn't care; she paid for both. Sophie did that a lot. She never asked questions she helped when she could. I remember being in Western Kenya during the 2007/08 post–election violence, and we couldn't get any airtime (phone credit) in the area. Sophie was in the capital city then and twice, without me asking her, she sent me phone credit worth Ksh 150 each. That blew me away because at the same time I had asked a college classmate (who shares Sophie's tribe) and he did not hesitate to remind us he and us were not the same, that we were killing his people, so he wouldn't help us.

During the post-election violence I was in the Red Cross camp, in the police HQ grounds, helping and serving the people. The place looked like a refugee camp in every sense of the word. The people there, about 2,500, had never imagined they would ever live such a life.

Their houses had been burnt, businesses looted and burnt, some even killed. All because they belong to the same tribe as the president, who had allegedly won the election. My friend Anna and I couldn't believe it. Sophie, on the other side of the country, heard on the news that we could not access phone credit and she again, without asking questions, sent me credit.

Sophie went through a lot of ups and downs in the time I knew her but she always got back up, dusted herself off, kept her faith and kept going. That was one of the most encouraging things in my life. I admired that and in turn it motivated me to pick up the pieces and keep going. I had the best times with her as we served in the seeker's ministry (drama group) at the church. She brought so much hope and normality in my life. Her love for life and laughter was infectious. There is always laughter where Sophie is. I looked at her and I always thought that is the way I would have turned out if I had a functional family. In many ways she helped me stay sane. And ultimately she introduced me to my husband.

I got a letter of acceptance to University, which was seven hours bus ride from The city, starting August 2006. Once again Dad gave an ultimatum. Go to school now, he would pay the fees, and then I can get out and do as much ministry as I wanted or stay in it and not have my fees paid later. I felt sad and, with a heavy heart, packed my bags and reluctantly started my university journey. I did not know that my husband-to-be was coming into the country two weeks later. Sophie met him as she stayed on for the year of African Youth Mission.

If only my new-found independence at university meant an easier life!

CHAPTER TWENTY

University life was great! I loved being so far away from home and having an independent life. I immediately signed up for dance ministry through the Christian Union on campus. Once again I was in a room full of men. Only two of us were ladies and in the next few months the two dwindled to being only me.

In the first few weeks I met two ladies, Anastacia and Anne, and we immediately became the best of friends. We simply called them both Ann and in unison they would both yell out, 'Be specific!' I started calling Anastacia Anna and the other Anne.

I had several other close friends. Frank, Ryan, Lilith, George, and many others came and went, but the closest all the way through campus and even post campus was Anna. I still keep in touch with the rest but Anna has become more than a friend. She is a sister. She knows my family like the back of her hand and treats them like her own. Now that I am far away she represents me when anything happens in my family. This is something I really value.

All through university Anna and I would show up for class and then disappear. It was not until the last semester that one of our classmates asked where we usually go. They had never seen us in a pub or club or any of those places and they were wondering where and what we did. They wouldn't believe that we stayed home. Anna and I had a saying in Swahili '*hatujakosana na kitanda*' (we have not had a quarrel with our bed). Pubs, men, clubs, drinking, none of that held any significance to us. We were free to do all the above but we chose not to. Everybody around us expected us to partake in these so-called college rites of passage, especially drinking alcohol, but we, without discussing it, decided not to do it. We were swimming against the tide as everyone else around seemed to think we were weird (they were a few other people choosing not to do these things but we certainly were the minority).

I do not think that there's anything wrong with drinking alcohol. Each has to decide in his / her heart if it is worth it for them not just for this matter but on all matters. I long decided it is not for me and do not think less of those who decide it is for them. All things are permissible (as usual in moderation), but not everything is beneficial.

Girls, just because everyone is doing something does not make it right! It is better to stand by yourself doing the right thing than following a crowd and having crowd mentality. Trust me, you will not die because you did not go to a club or didn't have a boyfriend by the time you are 20 or you do not drink. I have survived this long, so do not do things because people are doing it. Do it because you know it pleases God or because it is the right thing to do. Also only do things if it will be something you can personally live with and be proud of. Please do not suppress your conscience or the Holy Spirit. Let him be your guide in the choices and direction your life will take. Be independent of thought, let everything be weighed against God and his word and not your peers, other people, or the world. A lot of people define their lives by what peers, the majority, and the world is doing. Sadly they do not realise this themselves.

The year 2007 was a hard year for me. We were home at the end of the first year holiday, waiting to get back to second year in August. One Sunday evening, in the last week of July, I came home from church to find my step-mum and elder brother quarrelling. Mum didn't want loud music and she had turned it down, but my brother turned it back up. This went back and forth for a while as I was cutting vegetables for the evening meal.

Words like 'you are not my mother', 'this is not your house but dad's' were thrown around. I got tired of it and of course opened my big mouth and told my brother that he was wrong, and that as the wife of our father the house was hers. He should wait to get his own house to do as he pleased.

He burst into tears and kept telling me that I am always taking her side and to wait for Dad because he was going to tell. I didn't know whether to cry or be amused at all this. Was he serious? Well Dad did come in at just that moment, as he was crying and it reported to him. My brother told him just how I was taking step-mum's side. I will never forget Dad's next words. He turned to me and said, 'Do you know she will never be your mother? But he will always be your brother!'

I couldn't believe my ears. Mum was in tears now and was in as much shock as I was. I calmly turned to Dad and said that I wasn't going to take my brother's side because he was on the wrong. Dad was furious! He said we should pack our bags because at the end of the week he was going to give us each Kshs 1000 (fifteen dollars) to go wherever we wanted to go, as he didn't want us in his house anymore. We were a constant cause of stress to him. I was not sure if he was addressing all three of us with this statement or just me.

My mind was made up right there and then. I was going to leave and not come back whether he takes his words back or not. I was tired of the angry outbursts. I was tired of being abused and not having anyone take my side, protect me, or even ask whether I was okay. I was tired of pretending I was okay. I wasn't. I went to my room and slowly packed my bag, being careful not to pack even one thing that had come from my dad, even if it was a pair of socks. I didn't eat dinner that night and never ate another meal in that house until months before my wedding three years later.

The next day I was up early. I had to have a plan. I didn't have breakfast. I decided church was the place to start. I called my pastor and asked to speak to him. He didn't have a free moment but said he would squeeze me in. I walked to church and sat in the reception area waiting to meet with Pastor Nathan or Pastor Nala, the children's pastor. I had talked to Pastor Nala about the home situation a while before, so she had an idea of what was going on. I was there for a while and my tummy grumbled with hunger.

Three hours into my waiting a young lady I had seen and talked to once in a while at church walked in and began talking to the receptionist. She then sat next to me and we chatted a while. She asked me why I was there, and I broke down and told her Dad was threatening to kick me out and that I was tired of the abuse I had decided to take him on his offer and not come back. She was quiet.

She then said something that I would never forget. She told me that she felt like she needed to come to church on that day but didn't know why because there was nothing for her to do there. But after sharing my story she knew why she had to come. It was to talk to me! She told me that a few months before, her own biological mother had kicked her and her younger sister out in the dead of night with a machete. They didn't even have a chance to pack anything. They were just woken up and kicked out. They slept out on the street and in the morning started trying to look for a way to survive. None of them had a job but thankfully someone was merciful enough to rent them a tiny one-bedroom apartment where they had lived for those months. She had a job now and she supported her sister and herself as her sister also looked for a job.

My daughters, perspective is important. Sometimes you think you have gone through the worst things until you meet another who has gone through even worse. Dad had the right to throw me out. I wasn't his child! But this lady was kicked out in the dead of night by her birth mum with a machete! It is as though God was trying to show me that sometimes, we think what has been handed to us is horrible but it is always about perspective.

She then said she would wait with me and if I would like she would take me to her house and we could talk some more. She did wait and I did go with her. It was a tiny house, but I could see the pride she had to call it her own. There was a big queen mattress on the floor in the living area and a single bed one in the tiny bedroom.

'Are you hungry?' she asked.

Of course I was hungry. I had not eaten in more than twenty-four hours. She cooked some food for me and we chatted some more.

'If you need somewhere to stay, you are welcome to come stay with us. We will make the space for you,' she told me as I left that evening.

There were tears in my eyes. I knew three of us could not all live in that tiny space, yet I knew her invite was genuine. I was touched by her invitation and her generosity on that day. She did a lot more than feed me and talk to me. She reminded me that God does put people in your path to help you when it gets tough. She reminded me that even in the darkest times God does shine a light in and the darkness flees. I went back home and went straight to bed. I was still leaving Dad's house but now there was no fear. God was with me and had used this sweet lady to comfort me. I was going to be okay. I never saw nor spoke to that lady again. It is as though she had vanished.

CHAPTER TWENTY-ONE

That became my week. I would leave early in the morning, spend the day at church and would only return at night to sleep. My bags were packed and I was waiting for Friday for Dad to give me the money to go my way. If I had money at this point I would have left but I didn't have a cent to my name so I was at his mercy. I also spent the time applying for every grant and loan I could for my university fees, as I knew that I didn't want Dad to pay my fees anymore. I had decided that once I left home I would never call him to ask for pocket money or anything, even if I was starving. Thankfully I lived with my brother in campus and Dad had to pay for the rent for that so I didn't need to ask for that.

Come Wednesday I heard my step-mum telling dad that I was serious about leaving. Dad, in a very loud angry voice, shouted that I should stop being foolish and stop threatening him. That became his new slogan. I was threatening to leave. I kept my peace and didn't say a word. I had still not eaten a thing from his house the whole week. I occasionally had a cup of tea at church, but other than that I ate nothing. Of course this turned into another threat to Dad. He was angry I wasn't eating in his house but my mind and my body had completely shut down where his household was concerned. I just wanted to leave.

On the Thursday afternoon one of the church elders from Dad's church, who was also a relative and a neighbour, came to visit. I think he had been called to come speak some sense into me. I was called, and I went because I had always liked him. I always joked around with him and we were always laughing anytime we had a conversation. When

I turned up I was sad, shoulders drooped, eyes sunken, and swollen from too much crying over that week. I looked and felt defeated. Dad increased this by turning his head away from me and facing the wall.

The elder noticed this as he looked at Dad and then back at me. He then asked me what was going on and my answer was to ask Dad before bursting into tears. He said he had never seen me sad before and wanted to know why I was so unhappy. I knew Dad and Mum had spoken to him about it but I wasn't going to say anything, as I know Dad's angry outbursts, so I stood there quietly. He then asked me if I could go home with him and talked to him and his wife. I was more than happy to. I don't think he was expecting what I was going to tell him.

He and his wife sat there with cold food on the table before them. I don't think they could believe half of what I was telling them. I had been talking to them for almost an hour. They had asked me if I was hungry. Of course I was hungry, I had not eaten all week! They graciously made me a meal. They didn't get to finish theirs.

I told them of the childhood abuse in my father's house, I told them of the insults I had got from my brothers, I told them of the insults my step-mum got, how I was not allowed to defend her because she was never going to be my mum, and finally of the threat to kick us out and how I had decided I was leaving and not coming back. I went on and on in detail. They were shocked. They didn't have anything to say after that. No advice, no comments. I think my talking blew the rehearsed speech they were going to give this rebellious daughter of their relative and churchmate. They gave me a bed and for the first time in a week, I slept and slept. For twelve hours!

A few months later my step-mum, who had never visited me in campus before and never did after, called me and asked if I could join her at a café for a coffee. I went. We talked a while, and then she told me something that didn't shock me as much as she thought it would. She said the couple I had spoken to talked to Dad after I left and they had told Dad what I had said. The response was that everything I had said and experienced was a fabrication of me and my step-mum's imagination. He said that Mum had made up the molestation story and asked me to share it as truth to make him and his boys look bad. I knew Dad would defend himself in some way, and I was prepared for something ridiculous, but I wasn't prepared for the pain, resignation, and bitterness I witnessed in my step-mum that day. The story had turned back to her and Dad was trying to make her look like the stereotypical evil step-mum. For that one reason I regretted telling that couple the whole story. I would rather they had kept thinking that I was a rebellious young adult.

Friday came and went but there was no fare. The fare came the next week. I took my packed bag with everything that belonged to me and left anything that had come from Dad. I left, never looking back. Now I was in the hands of God. Nobody else would look after me but God himself. That was July 2007.

A few months before I had joined a website for musicians called Hear and Play Music. It was a community for people with a passion to learn an instrument, primarily a keyboard, and exchange ideas and lessons on the same. Of all the people I met on that site one became my closest friend to date. His name is Jack and he lives in the USA. Jack is a Caucasian with an African American wife and together they have four children—two girls and two boys. We emailed back and forth for years and in 2017 we will have known each other for ten years!

I got to know his family, his passions, his worries, his struggles, and his faith. I got to hear his wife sing at church, to know his children and how they were doing at school, and to see how a normal family lives, I guess. Jack became the father I didn't have. He advised me, listened to me, prayed with me, and loved me—my dark side and all. He prays for me in every situation, and somehow knows when I am down or discouraged and sends texts just at that moment to remind me that he loves and is praying for me. Jack made me feel accepted, faults and all, and gave me hope that there were great dads out there in the world. He showed me his great dad side but also showed me that even dads struggle and are as human as you and I. They have doubts as we do. They try their best even when we don't think they are and they have fears too. I came to realise just what a weight a man carries as husbands and fathers. They never talk about it, and many of them don't even show it, but that weight of being a provider, a leader, and the fear of doing it wrong is very real.

I told him about my family and my father, expecting him to make me feel justified in my anger and disappointment in him. He did nothing like that. Instead, he made me look at the good things he has done. He did not agree with the choices Dad had made or the pain I had gone through but he did not allow me to get bitter with what had happened. He reminded me with not so many words that dad was human and he too had his sins and struggles. He was trying his best even though his best was not good enough for me. He probably didn't have a good father either, and probably didn't know how to be one.

Sure enough I did learn that Dad's father was a most feared man for his anger. He was also a very proud man. Dad's relatives think he is the most like his father. He was brought up by a man who valued saving face than the truth, who valued family pride more than the condition of said family. A man who lost his temper at the drop of a hat. Dad was the same. He didn't want anyone to see him as a failure and therefore covered up a lot of things happening under his roof to save face. It wasn't right but that's what he had grown up seeing. It was nature and nurture working against him.

Speaking of nurture, I recognise a lot of Dad in me. I have often wondered why people would tell me I looked like Dad. I think they saw his character in me. I have become as stubborn as he is and his principles and saying have become my own. I have realised that in many ways I view the world as he does and when I make up my mind to do something, I stubbornly do it, as he has modelled so many times to us.

Here is a part of the email I wrote to Jack back in 31 July 2007, the very week Dad threatened to throw us out:

> 'I told you I will share in brief what happened to me this past week. Well, on Wednesday morning last week, I went to the cyber and sent you the note then went to church for our group meeting (we are praying about the name in one accord voices or in short, IOA voices. What do you think? And by the way, we have already been invited to several churches to minister starting this coming Sunday) and after the meeting stayed on to about 6 p.m. then headed on home. At home, I set about making dinner as I usually do, and my mum comes in complaining that one of my brothers (our second born) had been rude to her. She told my dad about it. He started quarreling everyone, threatening to throw us out by the weekend, but the biggest surprise was that the whole incident was blamed on me, yet I wasn't even there. My brother told my dad that I pretend to be good when he was around, but when not, I support my mother in harassing him and even refuse to give him food at lunchtime (never mind I

*am never at home in daytime) and many other lies. So if I say
I was shocked, I would be lying to you because I was more than
shocked. So my dad turns to me and says that I am not treating
my brother well, and that I am stressing him (my dad). I still
could not and still do not understand what I did wrong, and
asking him has seen him throwing shoes at me and banging the
door in my face. I finally kept my distance, and still am. Now,
the weekend is out and he hasn't thrown us out. But through it
all, I decided to leave home and live elsewhere because the stress,
heartache, bitterness, and anger this people subject me to . . . no
words. This is the last holiday I am staying here, and I have a
week before school. I don't think I will return, but I thank God
for his saving grace and for delivering me from all that. Now I
want to leave home where all I have known most of my life is
hatred, tension, and accusation. Anyway, as I have told you, I
am okay now, though feeling numb as if nothing else can harm
me, but I am glad to know my life is in his hands.*

*I was sitting in my room on Friday night, feeling all alone
and discouraged, when I remembered you and I felt much better.
I then prayed for you and everybody you have ever mentioned,
name after name after name, and I felt much better. And now
when I seem to be falling into such a depression of self-pitying
and all, I start praying for you, your family, and my other
friends, and it helps quite a lot. Thanks for being my friend and
for being my brother. As you can see, you also encourage me a
lot. Okay, before I end, here is one of my poems:*

> ### It is Finished!
> *All my hope is gone,
> There is nothing to live for.
> Everything is going wrong,
> No more reason to live.
> My future stands before me like a dark cloud,
> My past shining no brighter than the morrow.
> Nobody cares about me,
> Nobody is bothered with who I am or where I am,
> My life is over. It is finished!*

But along came a saviour, Jesus his name,
He declared his love for me long before my birth.
Loving me so dearly and personally,
For me he put down his all
And for all my trouble and pain
On the cross he cried out, it is finished!'

CHAPTER TWENTY-TWO

The last four months of 2007 were spent doing as many odd jobs as I could so that I could have a bit of pocket money to feed myself. I helped at a cyber café and as payment I was allowed to use Internet for free. I also began teaching salsa dancing in the town's only gym and I became quite good friends with Lucas, the gym owner. I tried teaching him but he had two left feet. In return he let me use the gym for free to teach and exercise and gave me the full fees for any of those dance people who came for dance lessons.

Lucas was a quiet gentle giant. He was tall and had competed in quite a few body-building competitions in the nation. He spoke slowly and gently and was a very calming figure. I will never understand what made him be so nice to me but he was. The gym became my escape and sanctuary (a very smelly sanctuary, might I add). There was no attraction on either side. We were just friends and he saw me as his little sister. I was glad to have a big brother. We never talked about deep life issues but we did talk a lot.

I wasn't a great dancer (I'm still not) but the little I knew I danced and taught with confidence and authority. I did get a few students over time and whatever they paid was enough to feed me for a while. I struggled to teach the men though, as I only knew the woman's part. Along came a guy called Mike one day. He was a young man, fresh out of campus, with a passion for exercising. He was a great dancer too. He started helping me with teaching the men and we quickly became good friends. I did have a crush on him though. My first crush, save for the ones I had for movie stars and people I had never met but on print media.

CHAPTER TWENTY-THREE

I wasn't going to church. I slowly started growing apart from God but still believed that I was a Christian. I was still in the dance ministry, and I would go for practise once in a while, but they didn't know what was going on in my life. I kept telling myself I was okay but deep down I knew I was not. I was angry at Dad and at life and even at God for such a crappy life. I just could not take it anymore. I decided I was going to be in control of my life! Little did I know that anger is a toxin that breeds sin and the more one holds on to it the deeper one gets into sin.

Mike and I taught dance for months. He did it in an unofficial position. He would only do it if he happened to be in the gym when I was teaching. We talked a lot and found we had a lot in common. I would go over to his house to watch dance movies with him. One day I did go to his house, as usual, to watch *Step Up* or something, as it had some dance scenes he wanted me to see. It was a Saturday. I stayed longer and binge-watched a few other movies. He even left me and went to town to run some errands. There was a knock at the door and when I opened it a girl—who could pass for my twin—and her brother were at the door. I quickly learned she was Mike's girlfriend and she was not happy to see me. Thankfully he came home a very short while after. When he came in I left because I didn't feel comfortable with the tension in the air. I had not even known he was seeing someone. And then to learn the girl looked like me was bizarre.

She broke up with him a few months later because she was joining campus in the city, and she wanted to expand her horizons or something. He was heartbroken and he turned to me for comfort. He cried for weeks and kept talking about her and how hurt he was. In the middle of 2008, months after his break-up, he called me. It was on 18 May 2007, a Sunday. Mike called me and said his friends were using his house and he wanted to come over. I was preparing to go to church but decided to allow him to come over.

He came and we sat and talked a while. The next thing I know he is all over me, kissing me. A very short time later I was naked and we got intimate. There were a lot of emotions going on in my head. I was happy with tears when I found blood on my bed, as it was evidence I had been a virgin after all, or to put it plainly, John had not torn my hymen when he was sexually assaulting me as a child. I was Mike's first virgin, apparently. We said we will never do it again but we never did stop as much as we tried. I told Ann and Sophie about it but as usual they thought I was joking, so I let it go. I would find myself back at Mike's because he was the only one who seemed to understand and listen to what I was going through. It turned out he really was not listening but pretended to, because of what he got out of the relationship. Now that was a tough time for me. I was angry at myself for letting him come in the first place, angry for letting him get this far, and so ashamed of myself for letting myself be a rebound. At the time I did know I was a rebound but it had happened and I told myself there was no way out of this one. I belonged to him now because there's no way he would be intimate with me and not love me. Oh, how wrong I was.

We were in a relationship for a year. In that time, I told him endlessly that I loved him, but he didn't say it back until three months into the relationship. I persisted though. He didn't even know when we started dating. When I asked what we would tell people he said we should pick a date. He picked June fifteenth. We had been dating for three months at this point.

He didn't have a job when we started dating, but got several interviews in those first few months, as I had told him I was going to pray for him to get one. He did get one but it was about six hours away from the town we lived in. Sophie and I helped him pack his house and off he went.

Before he left he proposed on condition that he would marry me when I finished school. He proposed two more times in front of his friends who jokingly asked him why he was leaving behind a beautiful woman when there were so many other men. He proposed to show them that I was his, and to ask them to look out for me while he was away. I said yes each time. These guys did look out for me and one became a good friend too.

I never asked him for a thing. I never complained I had no money or food even though I didn't have either. The little I got from the gym, the cyber, and any other odd job I did I would use to get phone credit to call him every day. Whatever was left I would get food. I had decided whoever I dated would not get a stressful, demanding girlfriend.

I visited him one day and somehow Dad, through my friends, got Mike's number as he could not get me on mine. He told me to lie to my dad that he was a friend of a girl I went to high school with. He didn't want to get in trouble with my dad. I didn't lie to Dad, I just said I was visiting a friend and he didn't ask any more details about him or her. That should have been one of the many red flags in our relationship but I didn't go anywhere. I knew I loved him and no matter how hard it was going to get, I would work at it. Life was not easy so I didn't expect relationships to be easy.

On the outside, I looked okay. My friends had no idea what darkness I walked in. I knew the relationship wasn't right. I knew the right thing to do was walk away and stop sinning but I did love Mike. I had committed myself to him and I decided I wasn't going to be the one to leave.

Nightmares of my childhood started coming back. Pain and tears I had not thought of or felt in years came back even stronger. I hid it from all, including Mike. I cried alone and hurt alone. Somehow I started reading erotica to make myself feel better. I could not access the romantic books that had comforted me years before so erotica it was. I would often read stories of much older men and younger girls through the internet as my phone had access. I started looking at photos and soon audio erotic stories. Finally I started watching videos.

The porn made me feel better for a few minutes but soon after the pain and tears of it all would come back in a flood. Somehow seeing these children molested, especially by much older adult men they trusted who were supposed to protect them, made me feel better. I felt that I was not alone and that it was a normal part of life. I was normal. They made me feel as though my experience was not unique to me. I was comforted by the ages of the participants, even if these stories and videos were all make believe, acted.

Nobody else seemed to take what happened to me seriously and nobody else seemed to care as much as I did. Most behaved as if it were a normal part of life. I convinced myself that seeing others going through the same would be a comfort to me.

Truthfully, at this point of my life I had gone back to thinking of myself being a thing. I was rubbish and good for nothing. I thought so low of myself. My mind told me that I was not good for anything but to be used by men and for their entertainment. I had no self-esteem. Seeing others in porn made it normal in my mind and heart. I was watching it because they were like me and I felt I belonged in their world and club. I understood those women and the role they played. I was one of them (though I made no money doing it). At this point if anyone had approached me to do a video, I would probably have done it. In a twisted way the only time I had felt totally accepted and needed by a human being was when John sexually assaulted me. He needed something and only I could give it to him. Now Mike accepted me and needed me because of the same thing. Pastor Nathan knowing all my three names was now a distance memory. That seemed like a dream.

Watching porn made me feel good for a few minutes. Then I would crave more and more of it, and that led to me watching more and more videos. It stopped being just the children videos, it became exhibition / voyeur videos, then rape videos, and then more and more violent videos—the last one being worse than the former. I was sinking in this hole deeper and deeper and my self-esteem was lower than it had ever been. The anger and bitterness was mounting. I loathed myself and what / who I had become. I was like a volcano waiting to explode.

I soon realised I was addicted to it but had no one to talk to about it. When things were going well I really didn't think about it. Immediately anyone or anything attacked my person, or I was sad, or had low self-esteem and lonely, then I would look for porn. It was my drug. It always made me feel like I was not alone, that the troubles and emotions of low self-esteem was not just exclusive to me, it was universal. These people would probably know how low I was feeling too, as I could see in their eyes. Though they seemed happy and joyful doing the things they were doing, I sensed the loneliness, the resignation, the feeling of being wanted and appreciated, and that, in a twisted way, comforted me. I was not alone.

I couldn't talk to my friends. They would think I was perverted. I cried and cried every time I watched them. They made me feel 'comforted' and 'good' for a few minutes but the emptiness and void I felt soon after was horrible. It led me to watch more to get the thrill and the cycle continued. I cried out to God more and more but he kept reminding me that anything kept in darkness will stay in darkness, and will continue to enslave us. He says to 'Confess your sins one to another' (James 5:16 GNT), but there was no one I could talk to. No one I could confide in so I struggled with it on my own. I was ashamed.

Many people think only men have a problem with porn. That's not true. There are many women addicted to porn. Some of them do not even know they are. Generally, women are not visual creatures, and though it is true that some are addicted to the same porn that men are (as some are visual), most are addicted to a different kind—erotica mostly found in romance novels. We are being encouraged more and more to imagine the guy of our dreams is with us even while we are with our partners. We are being encouraged to read more and more romance novels to enhance our love lives. The truth is soft porn is porn and we have to admit that a lot of us are addicted to it. We can't use our imagination thinking of another to enhance the relationship we currently have. That's like our male counterparts imagining the girl they saw on the street or on the porn video they just watched when they are with us. There is no woman who would like to be compared or replaced by an imagination. So why do we fill our minds with these imaginations and fantasies and think we are okay and it is okay for our relationship? I have been exposed to the so-called innocent romance novels, to the hardcore porn and everything in between—one is as destructive as the other. Just because we tell ourselves it doesn't, it does not change its effects on our lives. We can't keep pointing the finger at men and asking them to get help as we hide our own addictions.

Dear daughters, I don't care what the world tells you or sells you as a happy life. A life without Christ is a life with a void. And that void is filled with a lot of other things: alcohol, fun, porn, relationships, money, travel, and other material things. We all replace God with something if we do not actively seek him. Some of the things are good things but too much of anything is poisonous and so is anything that takes the place of God in our lives. At the end of the day when you go to bed, you will think of your life and that void will still be there. You will keep doing these things to get one more little fix to make you happy. There's no everlasting joy and peace apart from the one we get from Christ. We might be happy for a time without him but that quickly passes. We might even have a lifetime of happiness but on that dying bed everyone will have to answer one question: 'Is there a God?' He came to set us free from those addictions and give us genuine love, joy, and peace. You can have the most fulfilling relationships, travel the whole world, and still have fun in Christ and be able to sleep very peacefully at night. Filling your life with good relationships and travel, although good things, should not be a replacement of God in your life.

Porn sucks the life out of you. You will have a two-minute high but feel the most incredible pain and emptiness after. It is not worth getting into. The modern world sells it as such a great thing, as a way to enhance marriages and relationships. Many marriage counsellors even recommend it for struggling marriages. The world is also embracing erotica as a good thing and we see erotica books like *Fifty Shades of Gray* out, claiming that this will help the women in their most intimate relationship with the men in their lives. The truth of the matter is I started reading erotica as a child and I thought that it was okay. But when you open a door like that it is really hard to shut it. The fantasies take a life of their own.

God asks us to be pure in thoughts and deeds and to guard our hearts from perversion. It is not because God does not want us to have fun but, like any other parent, he wants the best for us and he knows the damage we do to our minds and body when we go against his word and instructions.

God teaches us to guard our hearts. He asks us to keep away from things that will destroy us. He is not a party pooper. I would not want you daughters to harm yourselves and that's why I do not give you a knife. I would not want you to get hit when crossing road, that's why I hold your hand when crossing the road. Does that make me a party pooper? I'm a concerned parent who sees the dangers around and tries to make sure you do not get hurt. God is the same with us. He warns us of the dangers of taking certain paths but it is up to us to listen or disobey and go our own path. When we do get hurt he is still there, arms wide open, to cuddle us and comfort us if we go to him. If you don't go to him, he won't do it, as God is not in the business of forcing himself on us. We choose to go to him or not.

It might look very innocent but the truth is it is far from it. The worst thing about sexual sin is that it is against our own body and it destroys us from within. We might lie to the world that all is good and it does not matter because we are not hurting anybody else. At the end of the day, when we are alone, we can feel the damage it is doing within us. The problem is the more we suppress our conscience the more it dies and it comes to a point that we do not hear it anymore. Just like a rubber band, it loses its elasticity. And at this point, we might tell ourselves we are doing the right thing by continuing in our lifestyle, but deep within, though we can't hear the whisper of our suppressed conscience, we know we are not doing things right. This applies to any sin we engage in in our lives.

Even though we read these novels and watch the videos and do not act on it, the truth is we sin in our minds. Sin starts from our mind, deed comes after thought, and that's why Jesus said a man commits adultery by just looking at a woman lustfully. Even though he doesn't sin physically, he has already done it in his mind. He has probably undressed her in his mind and pictured the whole scenario by just that one look. This, too, is a clear example of how no human being is good and without sin. We sin every day in deed, word, and thought and cannot reach God's perfect standard. Thank God for his mercy and grace that he saw it fit to take the punishment of my unrighteousness that I might have life everlasting, because I can never reach him otherwise. We are to guard our thoughts and in turn guard our actions.

Because of the added stress in my life, it quickly went downhill; and the lower I sank, the more I thought it was acceptable to do these things. After all, I was nothing and my life amounted to nothing. I was rubbish. And anyway, everybody was doing it. It was not until I reached the bottom of the barrel that I realised it was not okay.

CHAPTER TWENTY-FOUR

During this time I met a lady called Trixie who lived in my building and my floor. Trixie was 5'1 with light skin and always seemed to be alone. I befriended her when I was selling clothes on the side to make some money. She bought a dress from me. I called her Izzy. We quickly became great friends. She was much older than I was, about ten years or so. She was engaged at the time and was soon going to leave. We were broke together. We often counted coins between us, bought half a loaf of bread, a little sachet of margarine, and ate it with black tea. This would be our breakfast and dinner. We often did not have lunch because we could not afford it. We didn't know where the next meal would come from but it never really bothered us. I don't even know who, between us, bought the most food in the period of time we did this. Whoever had money bought the food.

That didn't stop us from being generous with the little we had. I remember one day meeting a very distressed lady at the campus gate. She was lost and had alighted from the public bus a town too early. She only needed about AUD 0.20 to get there. It was all I had in my pocket. I didn't know if she was genuine or not but I believed her. I took it out of my pocket and gave it to her. She thanked me so much and almost got on her knees with joy. She kept asking God to bless me. I wished her well and went my way smiling but in my heart I wondered what Izzy and I would eat that day. She had told me she had nothing that morning and I was saving that 0.20 for dinner. Now it was gone.

The day went on as normal and after the lectures I walked home. The thought of dinner came back to me. I knew if I didn't get anything we would be sleeping hungry that day. Just a few metres from my door I looked down and saw a $0.20. There were people everywhere and I don't know how long that coin had been there. I picked it up and looked around wondering if anyone had lost it and was looking for it. I asked one guy who had a little shop but he knew nothing about it. Nobody seemed to be missing Kshs 20 around there and nobody was claiming it as theirs. I then realised that God had provided because one of the people I had asked could have easily said it was theirs, but none did. That night Izzy and I added boiled eggs to our bread and black tea diet. She, too, had got some money and to us that was reason enough to celebrate.

It was not all was doom and gloom in university. I was a member of the university choir and we were given some pocket money every time we performed. Dad's youngest brother, who lived in the town, would sometimes give me pocket money too. He didn't have much himself and he had a family to feed but the little he had he shared with me. I know of days when he would give me his last coin and have to walk the nine kilometres back home in the dark. Funnily enough Dad's ex-wife, who hated me so, would also give me a bit of money every time we met in town. I was sceptical at first and very suspicious but God provided through her. These different incomes helped me get the most essential things and complete school assignments that required us to photocopy and print. It is also what helped me keep in touch with my boyfriend / fiancé, Mike.

As I had promised myself, I never called Dad for anything or to ask him for anything. Therefore, he concluded that I was getting it from men. He started showing up at 6 a.m. at our door in the name of visiting us. In my heart I knew he was making sure that I slept in the house and that no man had slept in the house apart from my brother whom I lived with. It didn't matter what I told him, he never believed that I never got a cent from any man, not even Mike. I never let him give me any money. I equated getting money or gifts from a man that's not your husband or relative to prostitution. I was not a prostitute. I experienced that as a child and I wasn't going to do it as an adult. I had quickly learned that a man doesn't give you things for free, especially money!

Even as I write this, Dad still believes I got money from men. He even asked Anna what I used to do in campus to survive in the month leading up to my wedding. I had told him over and over again that I did odd jobs but as usual he did not believe me and so decided to confirm through Anna.

This habit stopped one morning when he met a young man. He was at the door asking of our welfare and we were busy talking to him when the said white man asked to be excused to get into the house. That young man was Zane. I stopped him and introduced them. Dad shook his hand and welcomed him to Africa before hurriedly saying his goodbyes. And off he went on his way! I found out later he went to ask his youngest brother, who lived in the town, whether he knew of the white man living in his daughter's house. I was amused that he didn't even for a second think that Zane was my brother's friend. He just assumed he had something to do with me.

In October of 2008, Zane came to visit Sophie in Kenya for five weeks. The trip had been planned for a long while and Sophie and I worked hard to find her a place to rent so Zane would have a place to stay. I talked to Izzy about it and she offered her house to Sophie. She was leaving soon anyway to join her fiancé, so it would be no trouble at all. I was so grateful to her. It was the perfect place because Zane could stay with my brother and I would stay with Sophie as we were on the same floor in same building. That was the plan.

The day he arrived in the country, Izzy asked me to stay back and talk a while and let Sophie and a few other friends go meet him at the airport. She then told me over and over again that when Zane got there I should stay away from him and mind my business. She repeated this over and over again. She explained that the reason she was warning me was because Zane was a young, attractive single eligible bachelor and she didn't want me to be caught up in any drama, especially with my Mike or any of the other girls. I appreciated her wisdom and I purposed to follow it.

I met Zane the next day and after spending the day with him and couple other friends, we went to dinner at a restaurant in town. Sophie and the rest decided to go dancing and Zane asked me a question. It was also the first thing he had ever said to me. He wanted to know if I was seeing someone. Of course I was. I let him know this and that and he lived six hours away. He was silent again.

Well, life was straightforward in the next five weeks. Zane and Sophie would buy and cook food while my brother and I would wash and clean after. I did let Mike know what was going on and he was fine with it. I did stay away from Zane. I treated him as my guest and a friend but I never lingered or anything, just as Izzy had asked me to. Also as an engaged woman there were things I could and I couldn't do, and I was going to honour Mike through that.

Things changed though after Zane and Sophie came back from a weekend away. There was something wrong that I could not put my finger on and none of them was saying anything. After that weekend Sophie called me frequently and would ask me if I was free. Most of the time I would be. She would ask me to keep Zane company or take him to lunch or for a walk. Oh, how it used to drive me up the wall.

There was a time there was a bullfight on the university's cultural weekend that Zane really wanted to see and thought I really should be present too. They woke me up at 5:30 for a supposed 6 a.m. bullfight start. I kept telling them I was not interested because I had seen enough bullfights to last a lifetime but out of bed I was dragged. The bullfight didn't start until about 11 a.m.! I was mad and sleep-deprived! And then here was this white man insisting on getting as close as possible to the bulls to take photos. I kept telling him he was crazy, but no, he had to do the tourist thing no matter how dangerous.

Once again I realised I had been left alone with Zane. Toward the end of the fight Sophie showed up and asked if I was okay with hanging out with Zane as she had to go do something. I didn't ask what and agreed to stay with Zane. I remember walking all around campus with him. We even had black tea at one of my male friend's hostel rooms. I really should learn to say no. I still do not know how to say no.

I hate silences and Zane is a very quiet person. Sometimes I had to get creative with stories to say because otherwise he would just sit there silently looking at me, and he would be fine with that. For a talker that was freaky! I filled the silence with a lot of talk and most of the time I don't think I made sense. I remember one day I gave a speech about Kenyan politics and those who know me know just how much I 'love' politics. I was an expert. I also gave him a few Kenyan history lessons and I think he now knows more about Kenya than I do. I avoided personal talk as much as possible.

On the last day Zane was there in November 2008 he came to my house in the morning. I had just finished preparing myself for the day and was just finishing an assignment before I rushed to college for a lecture. He came in and sat down and after a minute or two of silence he announces that he is leaving that day (of course I knew that). Anyway, he goes into this vote of thanks speech for hosting him and all that and I thought it was really sweet! Then silence. I bend down again to look at the assignment paper I was trying to finish. Then he stood up and said, 'I guess this is goodbye?' I answered yes it was and I wished him a safe trip home, it was my pleasure to host him, and that I would really miss him. He looked at me for another minute before he said another bye, hesitated again, and went out. I went back to my assignment. It was not until years later that he told me that he had been waiting for me to hug him goodbye. Oh, Zane, you do need to speak up sometimes!

I could hear him and Sophie walking down the corridor as they left. He texted me his email address. Now in high school a friend taught me to never let a man give you his number because it meant that the ball was in your court to keep in touch, and when you did get in touch it would say a lot about what you thought of the man. For some reason that lesson stayed with me, and so not wanting that pressure I texted back my email before they were even out the gate. I smiled as if I had won but in my heart I knew there was very little chance I would ever see Zane again. Oh, how life proves us wrong.

Sophie came back from Nairobi after dropping Zane off at the airport. She brought with her Kshs 1500 (AUD 20). Once again I was mad! I did not appreciate it at all. I remember asking one of my friends why he thought I was running a bed and breakfast. Once again a man had paid for a service and that drove me insane. I typed an email to Zane. I couldn't believe I was the one to email first! I deleted it because I realised it was really rude and insulting. I do not know how many drafts I made but finally on 15 February of 2009, I wrote a calmer email thanking him for the Kshs 1500 and explaining why it was not necessary and why I was insulted. He didn't reply to that email.

CHAPTER TWENTY-FIVE

Mike sent me a text on 9 April 2009 saying he wanted to end our relationship. It was around 10 a.m. when I received the text. We had talked for an hour or so the night before going to bed and then in the morning I called him as usual to wish him a great day and find out how he had slept. It was less than twenty minutes later when the text came.

I was angry. I wondered why he treated me like such rubbish. One of the first things I talked to Mike about when we started dating was just how much I did not respect men who broke up with women via texts. I made him promise he would not do that and yet here we were. My first instinct was to call him and call him every name in the book, but in my heart I knew I was better than that and I would not stoop that low though scorned. Like any normal 21-year-old, I put my heartbreak as my FB status update just saying 'heart broken.'

I then texted him and said I respected his wish and that I appreciated him giving me the chance to know him and be with him for the past one and a half years. I then broke down and cried.

At some point I heard Sophie coming home and I went to her house down the hall and just told her that Mike had broken up with me. She looked shocked and all she said was that it was sad but he owed me an explanation for closure. I was disappointed. I wanted someone to comfort me and I did not want anything to do with Mike at that moment. Her response completely shut me up and I realised that I was probably on my own, even in this.

I went back to my house and back to bed. I did not go to school and nobody saw me for two weeks. No one came to the house to see me. They called, I said I was fine and they decided I was. I cried on my own, I was angry and numb for two weeks. Thankfully my brother had a lot of movies and series to watch. I watched quite a few of them.

Zane called me when he saw my FB post. He let me talk for ninety minutes. He called every day, he texted to find out how I was going, and he let me call him all the names I wanted to call Mike. I transferred all the Mike-anger toward him, and he never talked back. He just listened and kept calling and asking. Jack also called and texted me at this time; he became the father figure in this break-up. He texted and emailed and listened to me through this heartbreak.

Sophie came by one day. She wanted to borrow some salt as she was cooking and had run out. I gave it to her and as she turned to leave, she turned back to me again and said, 'You really need to have a shower and open some windows or something.'

I was embarrassed but at the same time it was like a slap to wake me up. I realised that nobody around me cared enough about the break-up. So I better get up, dust myself, and stop this self-pitying. Mike's life was going on and I better get mine under control again. So I did.

It wasn't until July that one of my closest friends, Frank, asked me whether I was still dating Mike. He was surprised when I told him of the break-up in April. But that question was a confirmation that to many it really didn't matter.

I was crushed by the break-up but it happened and that opened my eyes to see that I was slowly killing myself. I was dying alone and yet I had God on my side. After all this time, I realised that I had a choice. This was not me at eight, it was me at 21 and I had a choice. I had been sinning knowingly. I can't blame anyone for that. It was all me. It has been a hard three months but I had made it through. I made my peace with God and have never felt more alive.

Two or so months later, at the end of June, I wrote this email to Mike:

Hey Mike,

> *Sorry for being sooo silent. I was thinking a lot, and I had to get you out of my system and now you are. On Thursday night, I was awoken at 3 a.m. and couldn't get back to sleep. Then thoughts of you, my life, and my relationship with God*

came into my mind. And I thought about it all. Fact, I lost myself this past year, I lost my identity. Fact, I met a great guy—you. Fact, I met you in a wrong time of my life when I was not feeling great about myself and my life, and I was looking for love and acceptance from human beings. Fact, my relationship with God went down at that point, and I completely lost my way. Fact, I regret what we did together, but I don't regret knowing you. I allowed it to happen, and we both lost something by being intimate. Each time we did it, we both lost something. And I want to apologise for stealing from you. I am sorry for being part of drawing you away from God and not correcting you as a friend by allowing it to happen. I am truly sorry. That night, that's the message that was in my mind. I need to apologise to you so that I can go on with my life, and go back to the point I was before last year and go even further my relationship with Jesus. Honestly, my life is nothing without Jesus, and I was called to serve him, and where he got me is very far away and I cannot tell it all. I am crying as I write this because I realise how deep I was sinking without even knowing it. You are a great guy and I truly loved you. I am sorry because it didn't work out between us. Maybe I will never understand why you decided to break-up, but I am glad you did because it has made me realise I was not myself. I was just a shadow of who I am supposed to be. Hey, do have a great life, and I pray you will find what you are looking for and whatever you do, don't forget Jesus. Bye.

Strong faith or not we all go through some things that we are not proud of, but what we do after we fall is what is important. I have allowed Christ to clean me and I am still walking the path I should be walking. It doesn't matter what has happened in my past; what will happen from now on is what matters. It does not matter what you have done in the past but what happens between now and forever. Live a day at a time. And remember, your relationship is between you and God and not others. Your friends will let you down but never look at them to define your relationship with Jesus.

Mike came to visit about five to six months later so that I could hit him or call him names or whatever I needed to do to get over him. I offered him a hot meal and a (separate!) bed instead. I didn't ask why he broke my heart and he did not offer to explain. He had waited for the insults, the stalking, the questions, but they never came. Thanks to Zane, who had allowed me to vent on him for hours on end, I really had nothing to say to Mike. I wished him well and sent him on his way the next morning.

CHAPTER TWENTY-SIX

Zane and I kept talking after the break-up. He kept inviting me to Australia. I would laugh because I couldn't even afford my fees and I kept wondering how he wanted me to afford to visit Australia. To me he was joking but it turns out he was serious. Word was out that I was single again and so I got a lot of attention, especially from an African American pen pal I had. We had shared a love of poetry for a long time and now he was interested in something more. I considered it and let him know I was. It was a safe relationship because he was so far away, so that would work for me. In mid-June, out of the blue, he messaged me saying he wanted to marry me. I was online chatting to Zane when that message came. Out of shock more than anything, I told Zane about it. I actually thought it was funny because even though he thought we were dating, I did not think we would go anywhere. Turns out he was serious and I broke his heart when I turned him down.

Zane, on the other hand, was not happy with the proposal. He wanted to know what answer I would give. I decided to ride it out and see what he would say. I asked him why he was so interested in my answer and after beating around the bush for a while, he finally told me that the reason he wanted me to visit Australia was because he liked me and wanted a future with me. The decision was mine but whatever I chose to do he hoped we would always be friends. That's the first time he had ever been that sincere with me. A few days later we talked again and decided to give us a go. I told him I would think about it.

It took about a day to think about it but I made up my mind. We would try but the truth was I didn't know him that well to be in a relationship with him and neither did he know me. I also thought there was nothing to lose because he was so far away. If it did not work out—and there was a big possibility it wouldn't because of the distance—it would not be as big a deal as if he was in the same country where we would bump into each other. The relationship was going to be a test to both of us as to how committed we were to each other and our relationship. But I insisted that he had to talk to Sophie and tell her about it and I would do the same. We would only start dating if she had no issues with it. After all, she knew him before I did. He did call her and I did talk to her and she was okay with it.

It was not until mid-June 2009 that we started seriously talking about being in a relationship though and made it official on the fifteenth June. We kept in touch through emails, phone calls, and texts. Our relationship grew day by day.

We decided we wanted a relationship that honoured God and each other. Our primary concern was each other's spiritual life first. We decided to ask each other basic questions like favourite colour, music, about our families, and the questions got deeper and deeper. We also decided to study the Bible together. One would pick a book of the Bible and then, every day, we would each read a chapter of the chosen book and write a summary of the said chapter and comment on each other's thoughts and conclusions. By the time we were married in January of 2011, we had finished fifteen books and were almost finishing the sixteenth one. We were studying Jeremiah that January.

This built commitment, patience and love. Learning what we each value, our standards, our principals, and our beliefs I got to know how Zane thought and processed the world around him. And he got to know me too. We got to discuss our roles if we got married, how many children we would have, how we would raise the kids. It also got us to open up about our deepest fears, hurts, triumphs and pains. We got to talk in details on so many topics that a lot of people don't get to discuss before we were married. By the end of November I knew Zane better than I knew most of my closest friends.

In November he told me he had a gift for me for Christmas. I didn't think much of it, all I wanted to know is who was coming with it. He tells me that a friend who was coming through Kenya would be having it but I had to promise I would be at the airport at 6 a.m. on that last day of the year. One more question, how he would recognise me? And he tells me that he had given him a photo of me so he would recognise me. I was naturally curious to see what it was he had bought me for Christmas that couldn't be sent by courier.

On 30 December I slept at my childhood friend, Chloe's, house and another friend, Dan, picked us up early in the morning to go to the airport to get my gift. As we pulled up at the airport I jokingly said that I would not be surprised if it was Zane himself at the airport and we had a laugh at that. As soon as we went through the door there he was in the arrivals lobby with a bag in hand and another on the back. I could not believe it. He shows me a photo of me he had put in his wallet taken the first time we had met in 2008 and says that the person sent with the gift had my photo for sure. I was dumbfounded and that is a gross understatement. It was such a surprise—a good surprise. Nobody had ever surprised me before. I was thrilled to see him. I hugged him for the first time ever. I couldn't look him in the eye though. I had shared so much of who I am that I was shy and embarrassed to look him in the eye. Oh, how I had come to care for this man.

'I have quit my job, booked a flight, did not book a hotel, and I have come to see your father to ask for your hand in marriage,' he said.

If only he knew how much my dad hated surprises! I texted Dad on our way home and thanked God I had told Mum about Zane and our relationship two weeks before. The only reason I was home in Nairobi was because Dad was going to stay up country in our rural home and because Zane had asked me to get the gift at the airport. Dad had turned up a week earlier than I expected, Mum was left up country and here I was bringing a boy home.

We got there and we found our house flooded. The whole downstairs was filled with water as it had rained hard the night before. When we arrived my family were all standing on the first floor balcony. We said hello and realised we could not access the house. Zane, Chloe and I left, and we took Zane to the hotel closest to home and left him to rest.

I then called my maternal aunt, Hannah, to come visit, but did not tell her the reason. I also called my step-mum and asked her to come too. My stepbrothers, sensing trouble, packed their bags and left after New Year's 2010 leaving my brother, Ethan, and I with Dad. Dad then said that we should invite Zane to stay at the house because he was my guest and he should not stay at a hotel. I went, picked Zane up and brought him back to the house. He stayed a week.

At the end of that week, my aunt, one of her daughters-in-law and Mum came. Zane and I were called. Zane was asked to speak his piece. He officially asked my dad for my hand in marriage. They had no objections, apart from wanting to meet Zane's parents. And so started the clash of the cultures. Something that frustrates Zane and I then, and still frustrates us sometimes now. Our families and friends don't always appreciate the differences in our culture.

After that conversation I told Zane to pack his bags, as we would be leaving that same evening. I was not going to stay in that house for longer than necessary. I was already feeling like I had overstayed my welcome. Zane was treated like a son of the house and I am sure I could leave him there and he would be fine, but I did not feel comfortable being there any longer.

We left and went to Western Uganda to see the mountain gorillas. This was our first ever date. We were gone four days and being in a different country meant that I did not have phone reception—the interior of West Uganda have a different phone provider. We got back to Kampala and as we sat having dinner, I remembered a friend I had not talked to for a while. I was telling Zane about him and thought to call him. His name is Dr Willis.

If there was anything special that happened in my relationship with Mike it was introducing Willis to me. Willis is like my twin brother. We are so similar with similar tastes, similar humour. I am artsy but he is more scientific. Every time we spoke we had the greatest time. I called him and he was so excited to hear from me. H went on and on about how he had lost his phone and lost my number and how he had looked for my number everywhere. He even stooped as low as asking Mike for it. Mike was not impressed by that and kept telling him he was not giving him his ex's number. He probably thought Willis wanted to make a pass at me. I had no idea that in a few weeks this reconnection would be a blessing as Willis would help me in a great way.

We went back to Kenya and Zane came to my rental house just outside of campus. This time he stayed with my brother. I lived upstairs with a neighbour called Eunice, a single, older woman who worked at the bank. We had very little in common but for some reason we hang out a lot and talked for hours. Sophie had moved out so Eunice had become my go to person.

I was not feeling well. I had not been well since leaving home and I seemed to be getting worse. I got a phone call from my father. He was very angry. He kept asking why I had not been picking my calls and why my phone wasn't going through. I had told him we had gone to Uganda but that did not quench his anger. The next day he asked Mum to call me and tell me a few things. She prank called me and I called back. I was just waking up at Eunice's house.

Mum said she had eleven things Dad wanted me to know. And they were numbered. All I remember was something about me being very selfish and irresponsible. My ears were burning and my head was spinning. I slowly got out of Eunice's house, as she had already left for work. I was alone and I didn't want to be alone. I closed the door and slowly went downstairs, listening to the insults, as each got worse than the previous.

By the time I got into the house, I was so pale Zane says he was shocked when he saw me. The call ended as my credit ran out and Mum called back (she actually had credit and made me pay to listen to insults). She kept going. My mind seems to have blocked out most of what was said that day but I still feel the anger, sadness, shock, and resignation I felt.

I had done the most honourable thing a daughter could do to her dad. I brought the boy home to honour him by officially asking for my hand in marriage. Most others just run off, live with the boy, and come back either with children, or stay together so long that the parents conclude for themselves that the daughter was married. I was irresponsible? I was selfish? What exactly did he want? I wasn't taking Zane back home if that's what they thought of me and I wasn't going home. I informed Mum.

My health got worse and worse that day, and Zane was past worried. I could hardly lift my head and when he escorted me upstairs to Eunice's house he asked her to look after me. She took one look at me and the colour drained from her face. I went straight to bed and she stayed up for a long time. She was afraid to come to bed because she thought I had passed away or something. The next day I was better though, and poor Eunice went to work with little to no sleep. I purposed one more time to keep away from my father and his family. Nothing I did was good enough.

At the end of the five weeks Zane and I went back to Nairobi and met Willis. He and I took Zane to the airport, as planes to Europe take off at night and I was not comfortable going by myself. I stayed over at Willis' house that night and he and I talked for a while.

That's where I learnt that when I was faithfully committed to Mike he really wasn't to me. He was seeing three other women at the same time and he was weighing up his options. I was his third choice (at least I was in the top three!) and he had settled on number two, who just happened to be his immediate ex before we started dating. The girl I had met at his house that unerringly looked and dressed like me. I was so mad but surprisingly not at Mike, but at myself. I could not believe I had been fooled in such a way!

Willis, Zane, and I became even better friends. Willis was one of the groomsmen at our wedding and we still keep in touch. He became so much a part of my life that Zane's parents kept asking me how my brother, the doctor, was doing. I always wondered who they were talking about and realised Zane's family knows so little about my brothers (except Ethan) and family in general but a lot about many of my friends. When I count my brothers, though, he certainly is a brother. Probably a twin, actually.

I went back to campus and once again received a phone call from Mum with more insults from Dad. They were very disappointed they had not said bye to Zane. And for some reason thought I was joking about not taking him back there or not going back myself. I did not regret it. Dad refused to talk to me. He would call my phone and rudely tell me to pass the phone to Ethan who had just joined our campus but did not have a phone himself. I obeyed for a while but was continually heartbroken by the coldness in his voice. I told Anna about it and next thing I know she takes some money from me, buys a new sim card and personally puts it in my phone. I will never forget what she said to me, 'If I ever get you on your old number, you will be in big trouble!'

Knowing Anna, that was not an idle threat. I kept the new sim card. Within the week Dad had bought and sent a second hand phone to Ethan. Over time I was able to use my regular number again. But once again I was broken a little more. I didn't know how much I could take. My life went on. I was going to be done with campus in three months' time and I had a sick feeling in my stomach not having anywhere definitive to go after as I knew I could not stay in the rental house Dad paid for. I certainly was not going back to his house!

CHAPTER TWENTY-SEVEN

God does bring people at the right time and the right season. Em is part of the Navigators and was working in town. One of the dance members knew her and introduced her to us. She wanted to start a navigator's club in campus and was looking for a way to do so. I was the dance director at the time and thought it was a great idea to have a navigator's staff start a club in the school.

As a dance ministry we didn't only dance but we studied the Bible together, shared life and became a family. Every meeting started with Bible study and prayer and then we would dance to our heart's desire. I took my role as the director very seriously and I delegated different roles to the other members. We had a choreographer, another was in charge of music, another of photos and videos, another of uniforms, and then we would take turns in leading when we met. It was very casual but it ran like a well-oiled machine. I don't think I have ever led such an easy group before or after. The members owned the ministry and loved it. Consequently I loved it and knew in my heart that even if I was not there the dance ministry would survive.

Years later, in 2015, I saw a video posted on Facebook by the dance ministry and it had grown by leaps and bounds. It was such a big group and they still did the navigator's Bible study. Em, who still goes there once in a while for a navigator's catch up, also tells me of how big the ministry has grown. We had never been more than a handful while I was at campus. Now, the membership has multiplied and has a lot more ladies. I feel like a proud mother whenever I hear of how great the members are / were doing in their lives, seeing how much they have grown in their faith in God and what great relationships they had built with each other. The team I worked with still keep in touch, have regular catch ups with each other and they have been gracious enough to include me in their conversations. Praise God for that. He indeed took a little thing and turned it into a huge thing. None of us can take credit for it because it is so obvious a God thing.

We expanded our ministry to the churches around town and even went to the approved school once. This was something that had not happened in the previous years. We only ministered in the campus Christian union but I thought we could be much more as we had a lot to offer to the community. The community was also a viable mission field. Oh, what adventures we had doing this. I remember we went to one church and when we got there we found there was no electricity; therefore, we could not dance. Two minutes before service started we were told we were to run the service. Talk about short notice! So not only could we not dance but now we were to lead the whole service including preaching. They even cancelled Sunday school on that day as they thought it was a youth service. Adults came too because they had been told we were coming. They also asked us to sit right on the dais!

In those two minutes we regrouped, prayed, and planned what we would do. Because we couldn't dance we decided to do the next logical thing: sing (never mind most of the dancers were tone deaf). I volunteered to preach even though my mind was blank on what to say or do. But the Bible says we should be ready in season and out of season (2 Timothy 4:2 NIV). I prayed a quick prayer and asked God to lead me in what I would talk about. I took out my Bible to read a few verses as the rest quietly discussed the song they would sing. A few seconds later we were called up to run the services from start to finish.

The church was full on that day—about 250 people in there. There was no sitting space anywhere and many were standing at the back. One of us led the service and called the singing frogs, sorry dancers. Oh, we should have stuck to the spoken word or something. I'm not sure the key we sang in exists. But the congregation did not look bothered by it. In fact, they loved it.

Very soon, I was called to preach. I can't remember what I talked about but I distinctively remember the silence and the hundreds of eyes on me. The minute I finished and prayed for the congregation and those who wanted / needed prayer the electricity came back on. The congregation was excited as they asked as to dance. And we finally did what we did best, dance!

We had a lot of fun moments with these ministries and it did a lot to bring us all closer together, to be more of a family. When Em came along we were a family looking to grow even more in our faith and love for God. We were also looking to sharpen our knowledge in God so we could minister better to others. Em became part of the family. She would come during rehearsals and we would have a Bible study before we started dancing. We also started having sleepovers, movie nights and food, fun and fellowship (3F's) every once in a while. We met a few other navigators staff members in the area and that expanded our family even more.

When I finished on campus I started spending more and more time with Em and at Em's house. I do not even know how or when it happened but Em invited me to live with her. We kept going to campus to connect with the dance team and organised a lot of activities with them.

I lived with Em for about six months. Not once did Em ask for rent or food. I didn't have much and the little jobs I had done to survive in campus were not bringing in as much now. I relied a lot on the campus choir and the little allowance they gave us when we performed anywhere. Her house became my refuge, a place of rest.

That's who Em is: a generous soul, a wise and patient woman of God. She is one of the few people I know who would actually pray for you if she says she would. She has prayed with me and for me a lot of times sometimes on the phone or even on text message. She accepts all as they are but is very principled in her stand in Christ. She cries when she is rejected because of Christ but she would rather not have a thing in this world and have Christ. She encourages every believer to live a full life for Christ, as she does every day, and what you see in public is who she is in private. She doesn't ask others to do what she herself is not doing. Em has become one of my closest friends and we have had great times together as we encourage each other in Christ and through life issues.

CHAPTER TWENTY-EIGHT

On Tuesday, 5 October 2010, Zane and I got engaged. He was still in Australia and I was in Kenya. I had last seen him in February of that year at the airport when Willis and I had dropped him off. After that visit I was not too sure where our relationship stood after he had met my family. Dad had told him we could not get married until he met his parents and Zane's parents were not willing to come all the way to Africa to meet the parents of a girl they had never met. We had applied for three tourist visas for me to visit Australia to come meet his parents. They were all denied because I had shown 'no socio-economic reason' to go back home.

Zane and I were at a standstill not knowing what to do next. We couldn't move forward, as our parents—even the government—seemed to be against us. On this day at about 10 a.m. Kenyan time, Zane called me. I was out and about and I told him I couldn't talk much. It was also an odd time for him to call, and I wondered why he had called. I was on my way to meet a friend, then had to go queue at the bank and then go to the salon.

We talked a while about nothing in particular as I walked to meet said friend and I hung up to talk to my friend. Zane called again just as I was getting into the bank. I asked him to give me about twenty minutes and we could talk, so he hang up again. Twenty minutes later he called again and this time I had just got to my hairdresser's. And for the third time that day he talked around in circles and would not get to the point. The hairdresser even left the room and left me talking to him for a while. That night in the twenty-first hour, he called again and officially asked me to marry him. I was shocked (don't know why) but was excited too, and of course I said yes!

We decided we would get married whether we got our parents' blessings or not. We had both tried doing the right thing but none of the sides was budging. My parents had to meet Zane's and Zane's were not visiting Kenya only to come home and return at a later date for a wedding. So we just let them know of the engagement and then invited them all to the wedding. No matter who came or did not come we were going to get married in January 2011.

A week after this proposal Mike came into town. He called me, which was odd. I had not seen or heard from him in more than a year. I was curious as to why he had called me. He wanted to know whether we could meet up. I had no problem with that. I told him I was at campus just finishing up dance rehearsals. He said he would come pick me up.

Em was away that weekend so I had the whole two-bedroom house to myself. I foolishly invited Mike to stay over when he said he didn't have a place to stay. We talked like any two old friends about nothing in particular. He said he would have to leave very early in the morning, as he had to be on his way. I let him sleep in Em's room and then panic set in. What was I doing with this man in a house alone? Isn't he the same one who had said over and over again that there was no way the two of us can be alone in a house / room with nothing happening? I quickly ran to my room, closed the door and barred the door with whatever furniture I could get. I prayed that he would not get any bright ideas. I texted Zane and told him of the foolish decision. Sometimes I do things before I think.

Thankfully nothing happened. I hardly slept that night, though, and every tiny sound would wake me up. But all was quiet from Em's room. I was up with the birds and as a good hostess, sleep-deprived as I was, woke up, prepared breakfast for him and started counting the minutes until he was gone.

He chatted away as he ate his breakfast. Zane had sent me an email to check on me and I was busy replying to that. I was reading the Bible chapter of the day and was getting ready to email my thoughts as Mike talked. The clock kept ticking and yet Mike was not leaving.

Then he noticed the ring on my left finger. The ring was not from Zane and I had had it for months. I just wore it because I liked it.

But when he saw it he asked, surprised, 'Oh, you found someone to marry you?'

I was furious. How dare he! Did he think that I was so heartbroken that I would have taken a vow of celibacy because of him?

'As a matter of fact, I did,' I answered.

'Is he white?' he asked.

'Yes, he is,' I said.

'Is it Jack?' he asked.

Now I was sure he had lost his mind, and I also realised he had not really been listening when I talked to him while we were dating.

'Jack? Jack is like my dad, and he loves his wife,' I said. 'Why would you even suggest that?'

'Oh okay,' he says. After a pause, he added, 'I am sorry for turning you off African men.'

Oh boy, this man was really full of himself! He then says to me that he would like to tell me why we broke up because he knew I needed closure to be able to move on. I almost laughed. It had been eighteen months! I was engaged! He proceeded to talk for about forty minutes. I lost track of what he was going on and on about and realised he was trying to explain the reason he broke up with me when he said, 'And that's the reason I broke up with you.'

I was confused. I had no idea what he had just said, so I asked him to summarise it.

'I was in love with two girls. And out of the two, I knew you had the stronger self-esteem and would get over me faster than the other one.'

If only he knew how low I thought of myself and how low my self-esteem was, and had been for a while. How noble of him to sacrifice himself for the feelings of a weakling. I was flabbergasted. In all my life I had never heard such an explanation for a break-up. But there's a first time for everything, I guess, so I asked him about my weaker competition and how she was doing. He admitted it was his ex, the lady I met at his house so many moons before, and that she was in fact eight months pregnant with his child. He was around town because he had brought her home. As they were not married or promised in marriage, and he had made her pregnant before he had officially met her parents, he could not stay at her house and had to look for alternative accommodation; hence, here we were.

I couldn't help but think that would have been me, unmarried and pregnant. And pregnant by him! Oh, God saves us from ourselves sometimes and from our foolish choices. I was definitely glad he had broken up with me. Zane was ten times and more the man Mike had been and I was happy with my choice of partner.

At the end of that October I graduated from university with a Bachelor of Science in Disaster Management and International Diplomacy. Now I was free to plan for my future life and was looking forward to the adventures that God had set before me. I was excited!

CHAPTER TWENTY-NINE

One thing I had always told myself growing up is that I was going to honour my parents. I was going to leave my father's house in dignity. Dad is a very traditional man and I knew this was one thing he could always be proud of as a father. I was going to live an honourable life for God and my parents. They didn't believe that I was doing this at the best of times and I'm not sure they still believe I did either. Granted, I failed when it came to Mike and had a secret dishonouring relationship but I repented of this and was back on the right track. This is one of the things I shared with Zane when we started dating and then he surprised me by showing up to talk to Dad. Eight months later, here we were.

I knew I had to go back home now and plan the wedding. We had less than three months so I had to put down my reservations about Dad and our relationship, go home and do this last honourable thing. I told my friends from choir about the engagement and that I had to go away. I'll never forget how the Black Acapella group talked to me as their sister and shared with me their concerns. My own brothers (save my younger brother, Ethan, who had constantly talked to me since meeting Zane in January) said nothing, but here were men who had no relation to me talking to me, advising me and just being the protective brothers I so craved and longed for.

Black Acapella was a group of young men who sang African acapella songs together. They were also part of the varsity choir. Chase, Chaplin, Kalil, Leroy (the bass guitar as my in-laws started calling him for his deep voice), Monty, Olsen, Oliver, and Wendell were very concerned about the upcoming nuptials. I don't know whether they would even remember this conversation but Chase spoke out and said they would be happy to be part of my wedding celebration but were concerned it was too soon. They asked if could I postpone it until I was very sure. The others agreed and listening to them raising their concerns was very encouraging to me. It made me realise I had genuine friends and brothers in them. I knew then and know now that that they have my back. I knew there and then that though I had been brought up in a household full of boys and such a fractured relationship with my brothers, God had blessed me with many more brothers than I could have ever asked for or imagined. And not just this group, but the many more in church back in Nairobi.

Black Acapella did keep their word, and they did sing and dance at my wedding. What a colourful day they made it to be. I will forever be grateful to each of them for looking out for me and being my friends and brothers.

Most people have a girlfriend or two to take them gown shopping. My childhood friend, Chloe, took me once at the beginning of the wedding preparations but for the rest of the time it was one of the Black Acapella guys, Kevo. Kevo went from shop to shop with me and also for every meeting I had with the seamstress, Ellen. He was with me so often that most of my wedding service providers thought he was the groom! He did not have to do this but once again he proved to me what great friendships God had blessed me with.

Ellen, my seamstress, also became one of my greatest friends. I met her as I started planning my wedding. I did not know where to start and she helped me make decisions, especially pertaining to the wedding garments. She ended up going with me and Kevo for a few gown shopping adventures and ended up making my wedding gown. Her shop became like my therapy place. I would go to her shop to debrief and rant and we became friends. As a friend once commented, I seem to value conversations a lot and people who have listened to me go on and on have ended up being some of my greatest friends. I had very few people who listened to me growing up, so now I value that in my friendships. I also try reciprocating it as much as I can because I know how it feels not to have it.

Another blessing at this wedding time was Eli. Eli was part of my home church and had also served with Sophie at African Youth Mission. In December 2009 he had married a Dutch girl, Linda. I remember showing up from campus a few days before his wedding and calling him up to ask if he needed help with anything. He did need a hand in a lot of things, and was in a near panic because so much had not been done. I went right to work. On the day of their wedding, the ushers did not turn up, so Sophie and I ended up doing the ushering of 700 people.

Fast forward to almost a year later, here I was calling him up, asking him for help with the legal side of marrying a foreigner. He did more than that. He ended up doing more for my wedding than I ever did for his. He looked for accommodation for my in-laws, volunteered to drive them around, helped with the wedding planning, and on the day of the wedding, looked for a bridal car for me and organised the other wedding vehicle. Again God lined up people to take over when I was in over my head. But I am getting ahead of myself.

CHAPTER THIRTY

I said my goodbyes to Em, packed my bags and went home to Nairobi. I dreaded it but I told myself it was only for a really short time. Come January I would be married and out again. This was a chance to honour my parents and, in my own way, for thanking them for bringing me up well.

I hit the ground running. I had only three months, after all. I got my close friends around me and started the planning. Dad wanted a committee and no matter how much I said I didn't want one he insisted that we should have one. But instead of having my age-mates helping me plan it was my dad's age-mates. Right away I knew there would be trouble ahead. The committee members came every Saturday and, after a few meetings, I was getting increasingly frustrated by it all. They wanted things done their way and more and more the wedding was becoming theirs and not mine. Thankfully my friends kept me sane and helped organise a lot even as this committee met. I hang in there, reminding myself that it was only for a short time.

The week before Christmas things got out of hand. I was being asked to spend money on things I did not want or desire and my saying no made Dad angry. I wanted a church wedding but ended up with a wedding at a school. I wanted a cake of my choice but the committee insisted that it was too expensive and ended up paying the same amount for a fruit cake I couldn't care less about and it certainly was not in the style I wanted. Even the date we wanted was changed at the last minute, throwing off the whole travel itinerary of the Australian family. We fought over the invitation cards too because Dad and Mum wanted to send them themselves. I was tired about it all so I gave the 300 plus cards and left the inviting to them. Most of my friends got Facebook invites and heard by word of mouth. Unfortunately many did not make it because of the date or because I had forgotten to tell them about it through all the confusion. Fast forward to the day after the wedding and I found all the invites still in a box in my parent's room. I was so disappointed!

I was communicating to Zane about what was happening and on this Christmas Eve week I called him and said I was cancelling the wedding. I was ready to go to the court house and get married that way or elope or not get married at all. It made no difference to me. I was tired. I do not even remember a lot of the details of that time but I clearly remember the stress and the tears. Nothing I did was good enough. Zane encouraged me and asked me to hang in there as he would be there in a few days.

I remember the evening on the eighteenth of December. Dad got so angry after one of those Saturday meetings. He called my best maid Cara aside, gave her a piece of paper and pen, and asked her to write one or two things to me. He then proceeded to abuse me and made her read through what she had written back to him before giving her the go ahead to bring it to me. I scanned through the paper and was shocked by the words that could come from my father's mouth.

I had brought up the question of dowry in that meeting. I had made the point that Zane's family knew nothing about dowry and that I would appreciate it if they would agree to a phone call from Australia by talking to Zane's dad about it. I also asked if they would be mindful of the cultural difference because what they would do would affect me for the rest of my life. Zane's parents were only arriving the day before the wedding. They wanted to know what the dowry was all about and what was expected of them. Zane's dad did call, but Dad was very noncommittal and not willing to talk about it at all. Once again pleasing his community elders, pride, and saving face was more important than what was practical and what was considerate. I kept thinking that this was going to be a clash of cultures and both needed to compromise because this was a unique situation.

I was out of hand, according to Dad. She said that the reason Dad was mad was because I had mentioned dowry—an abomination for a bride to mention. I had been disrespectful and had crossed a line. I did not even know the line existed! He said that 'we wanted to be married like chicken, hence, we should refund all he had spent to educate me and then we can do whatever we wanted'. (My dad was / is always right. He still is and I do not think there's anything Dad holds close to his heart as he holds pride, his culture, and what people thought of him). He said I am very disrespectful to him and that's why I had stayed away after school. I had spoiled his name in Australia, I had miscommunicated the dowry to Zane and that he should just do away with it. Zane should give whatever he felt like giving, that whatever else needed to be planned I should do it myself because he won't do it at all. If I want to talk to him I should write down what I want to say and should not talk to him.

With hot tears in my eyes I folded the paper and purposed to keep it. Cara, Anna, and Faridah, my bridesmaids who were with me at the time, would not let me. I am glad I did not.

I did not sleep that night. I talked, I cried, I planned and dozed off for a few seconds, only to get up again and start all over again. It can easily be the longest night I have ever had. By the time Dad's rooster crowed I had made up my mind I was leaving. Unless Zane talked me out of it the wedding was not happening. I was up by the second crow, had a shower and was ready to leave. Just like three years before, I left the house without eating a thing.

As I opened the gate I saw Dad's curtain move and knew that either he or Mum had seen me leave. They had no idea that was the last they would see me before the eve of the wedding. I was heading to church that morning but I was not coming back. I did not know where I would go after church. I told the girls to sit tight until I contacted them. I would ask them to join me wherever I would move and they would bring my suitcase with them.

Willis came and met me in town. We were going to church together that morning. He and I went to a café to have breakfast, as it was still too early for church. I told him what had happened the evening before and how I had no idea what to do. I looked up my childhood friend, Chloe, passed by on her way to church. I had not talked to her in years, so I ran and called out to her. We talked for a short time and then in passing I mentioned that I was looking for somewhere to go for that night. She immediately invited me to go for a sleepover as she and her mum lived just a few minutes out of town. I accepted. I went to church happy and more relaxed. I did go to Chloe's house and spent the evening chatting with Chloe's mother. I ended up having the best night sleep I had had in a few months.

The next morning, on the twentieth of Dec 2010, I went back to town, called Eli who immediately got me a house, gave me some utensils and a few essentials like a fridge and a little gas cooker. I called Cara and we went shopping for other things we would need in the house. This was also the house that Zane and his sibling would come to stay in, as his parents and the family friends stayed with a family down the road from that house. We tried making it as comfortable as possible with whatever we could but at the same time we wanted them to have a true African experience and not westernize it too much. In many ways I now wish we had just let them stay in a hotel and have the luxuries they are accustomed to. Well, that's hindsight. The girls joined me at the end of the day and this became our house for a few months.

CHAPTER THIRTY-ONE

Zane came on Christmas Eve and we immediately set out to do the essentials like get the marriage permit, meet my pastor, and do our pre–wedding counselling. Most importantly, he convinced me to go ahead with the wedding. Actually, to quote him, 'My mum will kill me if this wedding does not happen.' That was all the persuasion I needed. You can't elope if your partner is dead.

His siblings came in the following days and I took them home to meet my parents who were still trying to convince me to go back home. Dad even called his brothers and my maternal aunt, Hannah, to talk to me to come back home. I went because I figured I did not have a problem with them but with Dad and Mum. I told them what had happened and how upset I was. I realised that they, as so many were doing, concluded I was just a stressed bride under a lot of pressure. Dad advised them and my bridesmaids not to antagonise me. When my best maid mentioned that the reason I left was the offensive letter, Dad had said that it was advice and it could not have been the reason for my leaving. Of course, I realised he had not told his brothers or my aunt about the insults. I did mention it and then used the opportunity to get into the house, packed all my things in a suitcase and wheeled it away as they watched. It was the 30 December 2010.

That evening Dad, through my best maid, called and said that I should not cancel the wedding, that I would see he had arranged a really beautiful wedding for me and that I should hang in there. It turns out that Aunt Hannah had spent the rest of the day telling her in-laws that she was not going to let her daughter get married in tears and if they didn't make things right she was personally going to stop the wedding. Dad didn't respond well to embarrassment and shame. I was going ahead with the wedding not because Dad had told me to but because Zane wanted to and because the rest of his family would be there to witness it.

On the thirty-first, the parental group arrived in the morning. They were to meet Dad and Mum in the morning. But of course Dad cancelled and asked for an evening meeting. Again things had to happen his way or no way (or according to those who influence him) with no regard to Zane's parents. They had not only come to a culture opposite to theirs but were also tired and jet-lagged after more than eighteen hours flying. That was not Dad's or any of the other guys problem. They were in his territory, so they had to do as he said. I felt sorry for them but there was nothing I could do about it. The meeting would be the first meeting between the families. It would also be the dowry negotiation. They were going to be really tired and jet-lagged and there was no changing Dad's mind. Once again I found myself in the middle of a culture clash. I guess that's what I get for marrying outside my race and culture.

We did go to Dad's house for the evening meal and before dinner the negotiations were done. Zane, his younger siblings and I sat outside, as we are not allowed in the negotiations. It went on for a while.

Both sides are usually represented by a negotiating team led by a chairman / spokesperson. Real food is only allowed to be taken after an agreement is reached. If darkness falls while you are still there, you are fined.

After the welcoming snacks are taken the teams sit in opposite sides of the rooms. Mostly women are not involved here. The formalities, the host's side (bride's) state their expectations. The groom's side state their position then the negotiations have begun. It goes on till the sides reach a consensus. At times there are breaks for the sides to do more consultations among their members. The dowry is always negotiated in terms of animals (cattle). After agreement part of it is converted to cash worth. In other cases it's all converted into cash.

After the agreement the groom's side then gives what they brought with them. An agreement is done on how much is remaining and the mode of clearing. It is an insult to the bride's family for the groom's side to give the full dowry asked, regardless of how low the agreed dowry is. This is a sign that they want nothing to do with the bride's family after the wedding and are showing the bride's side that they asked for too little. Dowry is typically a lifetime commitment.

Dowry is supposed to be a form of the groom's side appreciating the lady's side for all the work done in raising a wife-worthy lady ready for marriage. However, some people seem to equate it to payment / buying price of a woman. Surely no one person can be valued by money or animals! Irrespective of how much you pay, it is a show of appreciation. It is not paying for a commodity. A dowry is also used to keep the two families connected. If the groom's family 'owes' the bride's family then they will keep in touch. In my culture, when a woman is married she joins the groom's family, so dowry ensures that there's constant contact and the groom will be compelled to visit his in-laws once in a while to keep that relationship going.

CHAPTER THIRTY-TWO

Here is a scenario of a hypothetical generic Luhya dowry negotiation:

Dowry Process (Alice and Jeff)

First of all the two partners set a date for an introduction that is convenient to them depending on how financially prepared they are. The introduction is done at Alice's home.

It is during or after this introduction ceremony that the dowry negotiations date is fixed. However, nowadays some families chose to combine the two into one occasion due to financial and time demands to hold the ceremonies.

Material Day

On the day the Jeff arrives with his team / delegation. He chooses the number of people to accompany him. Alice's family welcomes them to the main house (her parents' house). As a show of hospitality Jeff and his team are then treated to snacks and some soft drinks or tea, depending with what the family chooses or can afford.

Jeff's team is then given some time to settle in and for some fresh air after the snacks to ease some tension, if there is any (a normal feeling to any man anyway).

The Negotiation

The teams are called back into the house where Alice's team sits on one side and Jeff's on the other side, directly facing each other. The chairman / spokesman of Alice's team then takes over the program.

He first goes through the introduction and other preliminaries about the main agenda of the gathering. After he has introduced his entire team the chairman of Jeff's team then introduces his battalion. The introductions are basically in terms of name and relationship with either Jeff or Alice, depending which side you are.

After he is done with the introductions he hands back over to the hosts' chairman. The chairman will then often throw a spanner into the works! He will say something like, 'Now, our honourable visitors from Jeff's side, as we are all now aware about our objective of meeting here, we are pleased to have this gathering so as to agree on the matter to be able to progress to the next stage. From our end we wish not to make it not in the form of a business transaction deal but a family bonding session over a pertinent matter. As we all know when a man wants to marry a girl like Alice, the family would ask for this number of animals, cereals, and other commodities. But because we are in a modern world today we would only wish to talk more about the animals. And having prior knowledge of our meeting here, we, as the old men who have brought Alice up into the beautiful and responsible lady you are interested in, we talked prior among us, and it is our position that as a form of appreciation for the great work done on Alice, you bring us fifteen herds of animals and cash price of Ksh 250,000.00 (AUD 3,600). That is our position going into this discussion. We wish to hear from your side on what your position is on this matter.' (The modern amount is determined by how educated the bride is, the higher she's gone, the more the dowry.)

Jeff's side's chairman responds and states their position and what their offer is. The discussion goes on from there with counter offers being made until an agreement is arrived at. They are negotiating. The idea being the bride's side would suggest a ridiculous amount and the groom's side tries to negotiate it lower. Back and forth they go. At some point it may get contentious and the two teams retreat to separate groups for more consultation between themselves. But it is meant to be a way for the two families to get to know each other and the idea is for both sides to come to an agreement. So if the groom's side disagrees with the suggested bride price they are free to counter offer and vice versa. It is not about the amount mentioned but the actual process.

Eventually the two sides settle on nine cattle and Ksh 120,000.00 (AUD 1,700), as the dowry, for example. Then Jeff's side discloses how much they brought in cash and the animals, if they brought some, can be seen. There is usually a goat for the aunties.

An agreement is then made in writing among the elders of both sides on what has been agreed upon, received, and the balance remaining. A modality of payment of the balance is agreed since it's done over time.

It is only after the agreement that it is clear you have secured the lady. She is then brought and presented to you officially. Food can then be served since there is an agreement and peace. After that you are free to leave.

CHAPTER THIRTY-THREE

So here we are on that New Year's Eve, sitting outside as the negotiations went on inside. Zane's side came out once or twice and talked for a while before going back in. Soon, it was over and Zane called me and whispered to me that I should go hug his mum who was visibly upset. I did. We then had a feast and talked for a long time.

It seems that everybody in that dowry negotiation had blanket amnesia. My dad, mum, aunty, my in-laws, nobody seems to remember what happened in there. None of them even remembers how much the dowry was. Yet I still feel caught between two cultures! I still feel my life after was defined by that one meeting. Nobody wanted to talk about what happened and most just smile politely and totally avoid talking about that day. It has been scrapped out of people's memories. Even my in-laws who had never experienced that have never wanted to talk about it. I learned that they felt like they were ripped off and I know my mother-in-law was overwhelmed by it. I do not know if they were or were not, as nobody talks about it and nobody tells me what happened—not in Australia and certainly not in Kenya.

Life for everyone else has gone on and it is assumed that mine has gone on too. It is easier said than done. I have lived all my life with a father who always had a preconceived idea of who I am and nothing I did ever seemed to make a difference. I could never scrape those ill-conceived ideas about me. And now I seem to have just exchanged one shoe for another. I am always on my toes trying to prove everyone wrong, trying to prove that not all Africans marry white men for money, trying to prove that I had nothing to do with the dowry negotiations, trying to prove that not all Africans rip people off. It is a huge weight on my shoulders. A weight I had begged Dad long before this day not to make me carry.

On the other hand, some Australians assume they understand my culture by virtue of what they have read on it. The problem is most of these articles have been written from a western culture viewpoint instead from the African cultural viewpoint. It therefore takes everything out of context and shows it as bad or evil. Why is the western culture viewed as the superior culture or the benchmark by which all cultures must measure themselves?

I have searched and searched and I have not found a single article or any information on my particular culture. Just because one "tribe" (actually nation) in Africa does one thing in their culture it does not mean all the other 3000+ tribes do the same thing. We are all very different even if some things look the same. My dad's tribe is Luhya, and his dialect is from one sub-tribe of eighteen sub-tribes. Even within those eighteen the culture around birth, marriage, and death differ. But it is a classic example of culture shock and culture clash and I am caught between both cultures.

At some point that evening I had some of my married aunties and my mum calling me aside for the talk and they talked a while about marriage. After this talk I called in my Aunt Hannah. There and then I bluntly asked her if my dad was my father. She was caught off guard. She had no idea that I knew anything about that. After a few minutes she said that in truth he wasn't. I asked her more about my biological father, and she did not have much information about him. She only knew that he was a Kamba and one of her sisters knew more details than she did. That was all I wanted to know. It was as though that confirmation settled my head and heart. 'No wonder all this is happening,' I said to her. 'It all makes sense now.'

CHAPTER THIRTY-FOUR

On my wedding day I seemed happy and excited and I suppose I was in some ways, But mostly I just wanted to get away and hide. All the tears and pain I had felt all my life that had been magnified in the weeks before the wedding kept coming up over and over again. My heart was heavy and burdened but thanks to a lifetime of experience my face was lit up. I had a big smile on my face. The burden on my shoulder was heavy and I knew if I did not put it down soon I would crumble. I thanked God it was all almost over. Zane and I look at some photos taken on the day and even he can easily point out the fake forced smiles in most of them because he has come to know me so well.

I got ready and went through the motions, my plastic smile and excitement in place. I had perfected the art over the years. I could look calm, excited, and happy on the outside but silently I would be crying and bleeding on the inside and no one would be the wiser. I did not really care on this particular day. I didn't care how things would turn out. If it was a success, well and good. If not, that was fine too. I would do it all with a smile. It was a bittersweet feeling. On one hand I was happy and excited for the life ahead with Zane but on the other I was sad and bitter about my life that had been before to this moment and this day.

We started the morning dealing with button-less wedding shirts for the groomsmen. It was disappointing but also I understood the pressure the seamstress had been under. I couldn't blame her. She had had to redo my dress, top to bottom, about four times. Every time I had gone for a fitting I had lost an inch all around. She was really angry every time and kept saying that soon I wouldn't even have a body the way I was going. I was wasting away, stressed beyond anything she could have ever imagined. I wish I would have only had the usual bridal stress, but mine was much more than that.

Then there was the case of the bride's jewellery that had mysteriously disappeared. Oh well, it was only jewellery.

A call came in from Eli asking what was happening with the cars as nobody seemed to be in charge at the petrol station where they were. Dad's committee had insisted they would take care of cars. Eli took charge immediately, fuelled them, and realised that there was no car suitable for the bride. He asked my in-law's hostess for her Mercedes, which she gladly gave. At this point I wondered what else hadn't the committee done and feared that perhaps I would not even have a cake at the reception. Thankfully the cake, though not my choice, was there. Truly this was going to be their wedding but my marriage.

Zane and his best man came to pick me up from my father's house, as is tradition. The best man carries with him clothes called *Lesos / Kangas*, which are traditionally bought by the groom's aunts on the material day. *Lesos / Kangas* are a piece of gaily-decorated, thin cotton cloth used as a garment by women in Africa. This is because it is assumed that by the fact that the groom's family is receiving the bride, no one among them can have any bad intention of hurting her or the marriage to their son. This is as opposed to the bride's side, who are losing a daughter! They then use the *Lesos / Kangas* to try to convince the bride's aunties to let her out. A back and forth game ensues of the groom's side asking and the bride's aunties refusing until they get something back. The best man and groom's aunties give out the *Lesos / Kangas* one by one until every aunty has one, or they are all satisfied.

In Luhya customs, and nearly all other Bantu customs, the bride is not supposed to walk on bare ground when leaving her father's house. Some use red carpets but that's the modernised version. In other customs the bride is carried to the car and this can only be done by her church-wedded aunties.

In Dad's tribe the bride's married aunties are the ones who then lay the given *Lesos / Kangas* on the ground for the bride to walk on. If the family does not have a wedded immediate aunt they look for distant aunts. The aunts also have to be from the bride's paternal side of the family. The bride's mother is not involved, she's supposed to be up front celebrating her daughter's wedding.

I have recently learned the reason for this tradition the *Lesos*, or carpets, are used to today. Mostly it is used to protect the bride from bad motives of witchcraft where some ill-intended people used to pick the soil at the exact point she stepped, then go perform African black magic to either ruin her marriage or render her barren. I personally do not hold this belief, as my safety and identity is found in Christ and not works of darkness. Initially they were used only in cases where the bride is a virgin on marriage day.

The *Leso / Kanga* are then divided amongst all aunties, maternal and paternal, married or unmarried. Priority is given to the married aunties, whether church-wedded or customarily married. The bride's mum can also be given a *Leso / kanga* although this is not really a priority. Aunties are the priority.

The bride walks out to the waiting mode of transport amidst song, dance and ululation from her mum and her aunties. Someone else is also picked to carry the bride's suitcase containing all her belongings and, traditionally, the appointed person would escort the bride to her home and help the bride carry the bag. The person is usually a younger, unmarried female, whether sister, cousin, or niece. The person can claim a cash prize to let go of the bride's belongings on the wedding day.

My best maid and I did buy the *Leso / kangas* for Zane and handed them over to the best man. We tried our very best to tell him what was expected. We had my friends, Willis and Frank, on hand to help too on the day.

We were late so Dad cut the proceedings and celebrations short, and ordered everyone out to head to the wedding—not that I minded. I just wanted the day to be over!

My youth pastor, Nathan, officiated the wedding. Even he did not know the full story of the heartache of the bride before him. I danced when I was asked to dance, posed for photos and I laughed on cue. No one, not even my friends, knew just how heavy my head was or the pressure I felt on my heart. I was slowly breaking down inside.

As I type this, my eldest daughter is going through the wedding album and pointing out everyone and making a comment, 'On the day Mummy wore a white dress and my sister and I were not here yet.' It brings back so many memories, bittersweet memories. Some good and some bad. On the day we had about 400 people, mostly relatives and their friends. A few of my friends did make it but very few Many did not come for a variety of reasons. One was because it was the first day of the year and most people are usually up country and, two, because many of them did not receive an invite. With all the dramas and pressures I forgot to invite a lot of people, partly because I just wanted it to be over with. I was sad I did not get to celebrate with so many other people but grateful for those of my friends who rallied around me and held me up through that really tough time.

After the many speeches, the dance from the dance crew and a surprise from the dance director, the day drew to a close. One of my uncles volunteered to drive us to our hotel. That night I slept for eighteen hours straight as Zane watched terrible movie after terrible movie (he still reminds me of how horrible these movies were).

The next morning Zane thought I had passed away! But to me a really huge burden had been taken away and my body just wanted to rest. I only woke up because I was hungry. After eating I fell asleep again. We went for our honeymoon to Zanzibar, and I slept a bit more. After our honeymoon Zane had to go back to Sydney. I remained to start the long process of spouse visa applications. I stayed in the house we had used to host Zane and his siblings.

In March we finally got all our paperwork together and handed it in. They wanted essays from the both of us about our relationship, evidence that the relationship was ongoing with photos, messages, or bank statements, two essays from two Aussie citizens who knew of the relationship, police checks, certified marriage certificate, I had to change the name on my passport, go to the foreign affairs offices and inform them of the marriage, and so many other things. By the time we were done collecting all the paperwork required we had a really big, fat file. It was March 2011. We handed it in and Zane also applied for a sponsored family tourist visa while we waited, as the spouse visa takes nine to twelve months to be processed.

I then moved from Kera to the west of the country, six hours away, to stay with Cara who had gone back there. The waiting game had begun. The call came quickly. It was April. The Australian High Commission wanted me to go for a visa interview. I was surprised at how fast it had happened.

When I got there, there were many more surprises. I was ushered into the waiting area and was asked to sit. A few minutes later a few came to the counter. They were talking among themselves and occasionally looked at me and kept talking. One of them was a white Australian while the others were clearly Kenyans. I was nervous. Anyone who has ever gone for a visa interview knows just how nerve-wracking and intimidating it can be. My palms were sweating and my mouth dry. I kept going over and over again what I would say and how I would answer the questions but on the outside I seemed very calm and collected, with a polite smile on my face. The little group dispersed into the back rooms and after about twenty minutes I was called into a little interview room. My interviewer was a Kenyan lady, and in front of her was a big file of all the paperwork Zane and I had sent in.

After pleasantries, she got right into it, not with the questions I thought she would ask but with congratulations instead. She said she was happy that I had found a man my age to marry, as a lot of marriages with foreigners are of older men with younger women. She said this pointing at my father-in-law's photo on the paperwork in front of her. She then pushed the file toward me and said that they really did not need all that paperwork.

She then asked me who was calling the embassy from Australia every day to quicken my visa application. I looked at her confused because I did not know anything about anyone calling on my or Zane's behalf. Seeing my confusion she explained that the high commission had been receiving regular phone calls from someone in Australia who seemed to be high up in government or something and had specifically been following up on my visa application. She said that they had had to put all other applications aside so as to process mine as quickly as possible. She said that I was one lucky woman to have a man who fought for me so diligently. I had no idea what she was talking about.

To further shock me she said that they really did not have any question for me but that they just wanted to meet me, congratulate me, and give me the medical paperwork. She then asked if I had any questions for the high commission and my visa application. My mind was still trying to comprehend what had just happened. Was the interviewer asking me to ask the questions? I didn't have any so she gave me the paperwork and asked me to do the medicals as soon as possible.

Immediately I left the high commission I called Zane to ask him about the mysterious caller. He had no idea either and six year later we still have no clue who it was that had been calling the high commission in Nairobi. Zane had never called, not even once. God was truly at work.

My paternal aunty passed away that April. She was married to one of Dad's elder brothers. I decided to go to the funeral. Many were surprised and shocked to see me there as nobody had expected me. They thought I had not forgiven my father, and I got quite a few forgiveness lectures and sermons. One uncle even told me to stop hating my father and start loving him because he really loves me. I tell them that I have forgiven but I need time to heal. Apparently, that just means I haven't forgiven. They didn't think that I had and asked me to go back home and pretend nothing had ever happened. I was tired of pretending. I was so wounded. I just wanted time to heal.

The only reason I even remember the above scene and many other things written in this book is because of the emails I had written to Zane and Jack when they were happening. I had seen Dad a handful of times after the wedding. I did not go home at all. I had put up with so much and figured if I was not good enough before, nothing would have changed just because of marriage. I was tired of trying so hard and yet failing in his eyes. He had long made up his mind on who and what I was and nothing I did proved otherwise. So I gave him his space, hence the 'forgive him' lectures.

CHAPTER THIRTY-FIVE

I did my medicals in late April and went on with my life. I was not confident that the visa would come through soon. It does take nine to twelve months, we had been told, and this was only the middle of the second month. At this time I was slowly falling apart. The emotional burden I was carrying was getting heavier and heavier. Throughout my life I had never allowed myself to process anything that had happened to me. I just filed it in my heart and braced myself for the next round because I had come to realise that the blows kept coming. No sooner had I dealt with one then another showed up. My friends knew nothing of my inner turmoil and struggle and though I had shared my story many times, I always told it as a matter of fact. It was as though it happened to someone else and I was just a witness. I do not know how many of them believed me or took it seriously but I know no-one really talked to me about it unless I brought it up. Even then I would be the one talking and them listening. I don't think any of them knew what to say or how to say it so silence was the answer. They too, I realised, had their lives, problems, and struggles. I felt guilty offloading mine to them so I slowly crumbled within myself with none the wiser.

Two or so weeks later I got an email from Zane saying my family tourist visa had come through and I should go to the high commission to get it. He then organised to come in the first week of June to say hello to the family, and to help me pack and carry a few things back to Australia. I booked an appointment and was back at the high commission a few days later, excited to finally be with Zane and see Australia for myself.

When I got there, my passport was taken and then the lady behind the counter asked me to take a seat. She called the Australian man I had seen before, talked to him for a while, showing him my passport, and then he disappeared into the offices beyond with the passport. A short while later he came back out, talked to the lady once again, and two more Kenyans (including the lady who interviewed me) came over. They talked a while longer, pointing at me and the passport. This time I was sure something was really wrong. Shortly I got to find out what was going on.

The interviewer called me to the counter as soon as the little group dispersed. She held my passport in her hand and, seeing my troubled face, said that I should not worry because everything was okay. She explained that though my tourist visa had come through, my spouse visa was only two weeks away to be approved too, so they wondered if Zane and I could wait for the few weeks instead of taking the tourist visa. She seemed quite puzzled and mesmerised by the whole scenario, as she did not understand how the Australian Government had cleared my security test, and therefore giving the go ahead for getting a visa, but had not yet received my medicals. She said that she had never seen security cleared before the medicals had been seen. They, therefore, could not give me that visa yet, hence the two-week delay. Zane and I decided to take the tourist visa anyway, as two weeks in government bureaucracy can translate to anything!

On the thirteenth of June I landed in cold Sydney and found Zane's family with warm coats and extra scarves for this cold Kenyan. What a great reception. Zane and I went to our flat that his mum had helped clean, and oh how beautiful it was. I felt really loved and welcomed. A family get-together was organised so I could meet the rest of the family. I thanked God that he saw it fit for me to join such an amazing family of very friendly and welcoming people.

With it also came a bit of weight off my shoulders. I remember one day my mum-in-law came to visit during the day and I ended up talking about my family and what I had gone through. As usual, I did it in my usual way, reporting it as an observer and not one that experienced it. I don't even know whether she remembers that conversation. I remember some days I would sit by myself and just cry and think.

Two weeks after my arrival the call came in from Nairobi. My visa interviewer was calling Zane to inform him that I had got the spouse visa. It had taken three months. What a miracle!

When I was twelve I started having a quickening in my spirit about my future. I had a feeling within me that I, to this day, cannot explain. I would leave Kenya at some point and would make my home elsewhere. I thought of it for days on end and had concluded that maybe it was for further education that I would leave. I started looking at schools in the US, as I was convinced that's where I would go. Everybody goes to the US or UK from Kenya, those two seem to be the most common destinations.

I was walking home with Dad one day and I said to him that I was going to go away to the US when I grew up. He asked me why I thought so and I just said that I had a feeling I would. He gently patted my back and said to me that anything was possible. But his face said a different story. I could see the doubt on his face and knew he was wondering how he would afford to take me to the US for further studies.

I spent hours in the high school library searching and researching universities in the US. I was going to go to music school and I had decided I would try getting into Berkley College of Music or to Illinois Wesleyan University. I still had no idea how I could afford the visa, let alone the school fees or ticket. I must confess that, that was the only reason I ever went to the library in high school. I had checked out their novels and they were not worth borrowing. I also could not stand studying in the library, it was far too quiet for me. I am one of those people who study better with a million sights and sounds going on around me with a break or two to dance or sing.

At seventeen, post high school, many people kept telling me that I was certainly not going to marry a Kenyan. I found it odd that they would say that. They had no idea why but something about me struck them as a foreigner's wife.

The most memorable one was a lengthy talk I had with a friend from church called Levi. Levi and I had finished some mission work and we were walking back to church. Out of the blue he says to me that he was sure I was not going to stay in Kenya for long, as Kenya was not my home. He was also sure that I was not going to marry just anyone, and whoever my husband was, was certainly not going to be Kenyan. I thought it odd but he just laughed and said by what he had seen of me, and who I was, he just had that certainty. He moved away shortly after this conversation and I went away to university. I never saw him again. Recently I found him on Facebook, and he reminded me of the conversation that happened so long ago.

Here I was in Australia, a land I had never thought of or dreamed of being in. I had thought of Austria because the Kenya Red Cross was sending some volunteers to camp there and interact with the Austrian Red Cross. I didn't make the cut though, so I did not go. Never had I thought of even visiting Australia! All I knew of Australia was it was the land of kangaroos and sheep. Not really things on my bucket list of things to see! It had all come true but not in the sequence I had envisioned and not in the country I had chosen. I did marry a foreigner, I did leave Kenya and I did go to school away from Kenya, not to study music but Divinity—again not a course I had ever thought I would ever study in my life. God truly does care about every detail of our lives and he brings people on our way to confirm the things he has put in our hearts and minds. It never happens in our time or the way we envision it but it does happen.

CHAPTER THIRTY-SIX

One day while in Sydney I contacted one friend I had made and wanted to see if we could get together and have a chat, but she was busy and would not be free for the next three weeks. I remember how alone I felt. I realised I had come into a culture where everything is measured by time and through a diary. I was becoming increasingly frustrated that I needed to book an appointment to see a friend. I kept wondering what would happen if it was an emergency. I was so used to Kenyans who I would call and they would make sure to see me either by the end of the day or within the next twenty-four hours or if they were far away. Back home relationships and people are more important than time, but in my new land time seemed more important to many people. My relationships in Kenya were never (and still aren't) measured by time, and this would irritate an Australian to no end.

I quickly learned that I had to make my own path and look for the exceptions, the friends who would give me the time of the day. I also had to be okay with being alone if I could not find one. I must confess that I have since learned not to call anyone. I figure if God was able to see me through very lonely and painful years he can continually do that even in Australia. I am mostly at a loss as to what is culturally acceptable in this foreign land I find myself, so I choose to stay back and watch. One day I will belong and will feel like I understand it and I am a part of it. But for now, I'll watch and hopefully learn.

I also kept in touch with my many friends back home and they really helped to hold me together for the three months I was in Australia. I went back after the three months to get the permanent visa, say my final goodbyes, pack the rest of my things in Kenya and move to Australia for good. The next time we would be there would be in 2013 with our 4-month-old daughter.

I came back into the country on 15 October 2011. We had moved a little further north of Sydney, NSW. Once again it was going to be a new start for me. Thankfully Zane had a cousin and her family who lived in the same suburb and were within walking distance. I loved Newcastle straight away. I had always been a small town girl, cities are such a stressful place for me. I only went to cities if I absolutely had to. I found Sydney very stressful and not very communal. I longed for community and I found that and some more in Newcastle.

My first surprise came on my first day in Newcastle. My immediate neighbour came knocking on my door, welcomed me, and gave me some dinner. She was an Indian lady, a Sikh. I was really surprised. Coming from Kenya, I had not had very good interactions with Indians, especially with Sikhs. They were not the friendliest people, especially to Africans, and they kept their distance. Despite the fact that Indians have been in Kenya since 1900, there's very little or no interactions with the indigenous people, mostly because of their caste system.

But here was a Sikh woman who knew nothing about me, coming into my house, and even making us dinner. I was pleasantly surprised. We continued to be very good friends and shared quite a few cups of tea in her house and my house. I learned a most valuable lesson from her. No matter what a group of people does or what their culture is, they are also individuals. Don't judge them by their culture, religion, or race. Judge them as individuals. There are good and bad people in every people grouping, so blanket conclusions are not warranted. In the same way, I pray that I, too, will stop being judged as a money-hungry African. I know a few people who marry for money but they are not exclusively African and neither are they exclusively from a third world country. There are those kinds of people in every society, every socio-economic class and people grouping.

CHAPTER THIRTY-SEVEN

Zane worked long hours, from the crack of dawn to late evening. I missed home, my culture, and even speaking Swahili. I had a lot of time to think and analyse every little thing. I had finally put the burden down and was going through the content. The panic attacks started at this time. They were sporadic. Something would trigger them and I would be curled up into a ball, struggling to breathe. Then the unstoppable tears would start. I was a mess.

Zane would touch me and off I would go into my head and start panicking. I would see John's face and would relive every single thing he did to me. Zane would hold me and repeat over and over again that it was just him and nobody would harm me again. He would keep reminding me to breathe. This would last a few seconds and sometimes minutes but it would always be followed with tears and pain so deep within that I can't explain in words.

The porn multiplied tenfold. I had not thought of it nor looked at it since Mike. But once again I was feeling so low and sorry for myself and the porn came back. I had thought I had dealt with it but realised that when I was low and had low self-esteem, the temptation came back. In my mind, porn made me feel better. It helped me forget and became my pain killer and confirmed to me that I was still human and normal. That what happened to me is a normal part of life. I mean, the porn industry and its subscribers shows just how big the industry and demand is so, to me then, I should not be taking my life experience as a child too personally as it was normal.

I hid it for a while out of shame and embarrassment but quickly realised whatever is kept in darkness multiplies. I gathered my courage and told Zane about it. He was gracious and he prayed for and with me. And every time during the day I would get a panic attack or be tempted I would call him at work or text him and he would talk to me for a while until I felt better. He still calls me every day at lunchtime to make sure I am doing okay.

The Bible does say to 'confess our sins one to another so that you may be healed' in James 5:16 (GNB). Keeping our sins and struggles a secret only makes it worse and we remain in the darkness, but sharing it with someone you trust and one who will not judge you but pray for you will bring it to the light and consequently bring healing and freedom. I so desperately sought that freedom because I was tired, and my heart was heavy with sadness.

I had also realised that everybody's life in my motherland was moving on and yet I was holding on to memories and experiences we had together. One of my friend's mum told me plainly that I had to live in my present reality and had to grow where God had planted me. I realised just how invested I had been to my relationships in Kenya and not too much in those around me in Australia. This was further confirmed when I had a fall out with my best friend of twelve years—a friendship that has never recovered since.

Zane and I were also being asked if we would have an Australian wedding so those who had not been able to come to Kenya could witness too. I kept postponing it but eventually we decided to have a celebratory reception in Sydney on the third of March 2012 instead and invited family and friends. I was not going to have another wedding. One was enough for me with all the pain and frustrations that came with it.

I got pregnant at around this time and the journey to motherhood begun. I was excited and happy, but also very anxious and nervous. The panic attacks increased and were more frequent and more intense as I kept asking myself what I would if it was a little girl. I would not want my daughter to go through what I did. I would do anything to protect my little girl. Then the fear of my child being brought up without their parent came up. I remember telling Zane more than once that if anything happened to me, he should promise to be very careful who looks after our child and if he ever remarries, he should be very careful whom he marries because I was paranoid as to who would bring up my child. Zane kept saying I should seek help as I seemed to be getting worse.

A lot of people over the years ask why I did not seek help. I was not taught to seek help, I was taught to ignore the things that happen—to let bygones be bygones. There seems to be wisdom in those words but it just encourages people not to deal with unresolved issues and those who try to are viewed as weak or unforgiving. Forgive and forget has been drummed into me. When I talk about it I am told that I have not forgiven. I don't believe that. I, from experience, know that even if I have forgiven the pain remains for a while.

Forgiveness, to me, means choosing not to be the judge in the person's life; it means I stop playing God over them. And truly I do not judge those who hurt me but my mind, heart and body needs to deal with the emotions and pain caused by the hurt. I talk about it as a way to deal with it. Keeping it inside is like ignoring a cancer that keeps growing and that's what happened to me. Telling people to ignore what has happened in their lives is not helping them and dismissing it as something that happened a long time ago or is a normal part of life makes it worse for the person. It makes them feel belittled, alone, petty, and ignored. And yet the feelings are real, the pain is in real time, the nightmares are a part of their lives, and the events affect every aspect of their lives for the rest of their lives.

For me, my experiences affect my present reality, my trusting others, my marriage, my parenting, my friendships. I have moments I would not allow Zane anywhere near me because it makes me panic. Sometimes I am paranoid about my girls' safety and want to protect them from every man, as I would not want them to experience what I did. Then there are moments I want nothing to do with anyone and just stay in the house and cry.

I called a lovely lady from church called Julie. Julie had been taking me to my appointments as I was not driving yet and she picked me up for Bible study every week too. I talked to her and told her what was going on and she listened and spent some time talking to me and reassuring me. She pointed out that the fact I was pregnant was a big contributing factor to my emotions getting worse because as a parent I was fearful of my life events happening to my child. She reminded me that my child was not me and my child will have her own life and her own challenges. She reminded me I was not my mother. It seems like such a simple concept but it was very profound to me at that moment.

She kept telling me I needed to forgive those who have hurt me. And I kept saying that I had forgiven them but I still felt intense pain every time I thought about them and the situation. I realised that the wedding had scratched the scars I had and they were now fresh wounds. I had not dealt with the new wounds. I was still holding on to the anger and pain and the more I thought about it, the more I was scratching into more scars and reopening old wounds. No wonder I was losing it.

She also asked me to forgive my mum for abandoning me. I had never thought of that. I knew she had not abandoned me, she died. But I did feel abandoned by that single event. I was also to forgive myself for thinking that Mum had abandoned me, for thinking so low of myself and allowing myself to continually do so. Julie left me with a lot to think about and I did seriously think about it. I did pray and things settled for a while. I can pin point this one conversation as one of the most significant conversation in my healing journey.

That December, through C-section, the most beautiful girl was born. We named her Sarah. Her first name means light and Sarah was my mum's name. She has Sarah's hair and, according to Aunt Hannah, she has Mum's personality too. She really brought light into my dark world and with that light came healing in some part of my life. But the fight was far from done.

Two years and eight months later we had another lovely girl and named her Grace. Her first name means beauty in Swahili, golden thread in Indian, and golden in Persian and Arabic. She shows me the beauty of God's grace every day and shows the golden thread of God's grace that has been woven through my life. The world may only see the pain and hard times but God has shown me the beauty and the golden thread in the most painful moments and in the moments I was at my lowest. The tapestry of my life has been threaded with the most beautiful golden thread of grace even when I did not think God was there in some situations. And now standing back and looking back I see the most beautiful tapestry and I would not change a thing in it. I praise God for each of those moments of grace. Surely, his grace is sufficient!

The name Grace is from her paternal great-grandmother who passed away long ago when her grandma was fourteen. Grace was also the name of my mum, Sarah's, cousin who was also her best friend.

My little Grace has my mum, Sarah's, teeth and smile, my eyes, and my Grandma Esther's cheeks. She is a peaceful, patient child, and Aunt Hannah mentioned Grandmother Esther was much the same.

These two remind me every day of God's light and God's beauty. Oh, how God has blessed me. Both Sarah and her mum, Esther, were strong women of faith and what a privilege to be the mother of two little girls who are much like they were. It is as though God is giving me a chance to know more about my mum and grandmum—two women I so longed to know. God's healing me through these two every day.

Over the next two years, I made new friends and they have been there for us through thick and thin. Most of these friends are friends from the Bible studies we attend. They have helped us move three times, helped us renovate a house, prayed with us, helped financially when we we're struggling and given us a place to stay when we had no shelter. God has blessed me with such a beautiful community and, where I lacked mothers and fathers, God has given me tenfold. Where I lacked sisters, he has given me more than I could have asked or imagined. Where I lacked love and acceptance, he has given me a large family here in Newcastle that love me as I am. They care about where I came from, where I am and where I am going. They frequently ask about my family and friends back home, and even once gave financially to help my dad when he was in need. Zane and I and the girls feel loved and accepted by these people. We feel that we are home with them. My eldest daughter calls most of them grandparents (each couple with their own nickname), and she is convinced they are family and loves each of them as she does her own grandparents.

CHAPTER THIRTY-EIGHT

I called Aunt Hannah once and asked her about Mum's last days. She was with Mum those last days in hospital. Hannah told me that Mum said, 'I have given birth like a *mzungu* (*mzungu* is Swahili for white person), but that is okay because I know my girl will grow up and look after her brother.' She, according to Aunt Hannah, was very confident in her last word. She was happy too and very calm and peaceful.

She said that because Africans believe whites have one or two children, while in Africa children are a thing of pride; the more you have the more respected one is. Unfortunately the world economic system does not allow this anymore.

Mum then said that she was sure I will marry a good, kind man who will take care of me and she would die peacefully knowing that my brother and I would be okay from what she had seen in our futures. Mum also asked Aunty Hannah to take her place and raise me but Dad totally opposed that after the funeral. Mum wanted her sister to adopt me. The most encouraging part of this story is that Mum had seen my future and I believe it was God himself showing her so that she would not worry about us. She died joyfully and with peace that can only come from God. Zane is every bit the man Mum described and I know she is proud and glad that God did make his promise to her come to pass.

At this point Aunty Hannah rightly points out that if she had brought me up I would not have finished school, as she had no means to even educate her own children. I would have probably been married much younger. She reminded me that no matter how bad dad was, he had done a great job of making sure I went all the way to university and had brought me up to be principled and focused.

For the first time ever I told her of exactly what had been happening to me in Dad's house. She was shocked and hurt by it all but, like many others, asked me to let bygones be bygones and forgive and move on.

I asked Aunt Hannah about my biological father one more time in early 2016. She informed me that she had learnt he had died a few years before. I mourned for the father I did not know and for the life that wasn't but could have been. I also mourned for the lost chance to meet him and find out what happened. She didn't know his name, and neither do I. Nobody seems to care enough about this matter; it only seems to matter to me. Hannah was surprised about that and wondered why I would waste my tears on him. I realised that this was a burden only people who were adopted from single parent families, where one of the partners left or who were brought up by people who are not their biological parents, would understand. We struggle to know who we are and to feel fully accepted because of the feeling of abandonment created by the void left by the parent who left. We just want to know where we came from and why the people we share DNA with abandoned us. We are not asking for a relationship with these strangers we share blood with (though if it comes, it is a bonus). Neither are we saying that those who brought us up were terrible. It is just our hearts wanting to know our origin and where we belong.

I once heard on a video I was watching that psychologists say that a mother nurtures a child but it is a father that calls forth the woman or man in them. When we are growing up we want our identity to be known; we want to understand who we are. If there's been a lack of definition in our lives, if there's been abuse or neglect, we get mixed up. We all long for the love of a father and the nurturing of a mother.

I longed for the love of a father most of all, and in many ways, I still do. I searched for that love, acceptance, and affirmation all my life, but instead, I received criticism and insults. I was never good enough. I longed for a father to embrace me and protect me, but I did not get that either.

My dad has never apologised nor has he ever acknowledged what happened to me over the last few decades, but we are on speaking terms and I would dare say, friends. I believe, in his own way, he is sorry. But as I said before he is a man full of pride by nature and nurture, and things like apologies and admitting he is wrong are not natural to him. He has turned his life around and for the first time ever I see the man of faith. He and I sometimes talk for two hours on the phone. We laugh and make jokes, and he even asks my opinion on different things—something that still shocks me! Most conversations end with him encouraging me with God's word. Sometimes his old self shows up but then I see he is trying to be a better father, and I am going to let him. God has given me a second chance once too many a times. Who am I to deny my fellow human the same? He, God, is the only one who knows the heart of man, and therefore is the only one who can judge my dad's heart.

I love my dad and I will continue to honour him. This book is not meant to make him to look like a bad man but it is a story of my experience and my memories. It is a story that shows human beings in all their weaknesses and failings. We all have those. Dad is human, and he has made bad choices. If I carry hate and anger, I, too, might do the same things he has done—or worse. The 'log' in one's eye is usually big and blinding, so let the 'speck' of your neighbour's eye be as you first remove the 'log' in yours. Far be it that someone calls me righteous or good. I am neither. Only God is good and righteous. I fail like any other person. And when I do fail, I pray that I will be forgiven. That's why Christ came, because we are all sinners. 'Let him without sin throw the first stone,' Jesus said. I have my fair share of failings and God has forgiven me for those, and I therefore will extend the courtesy to others.

I will fail you too, my dear girls, in one way or another. As long as we are on this earth, perfection will not be attained. But, by faith, we will be made perfect with Christ in the fullness of time. No one is perfect, not even one. None is good either as much as we tell ourselves we are good people, only God is good. I pray that you, too, will find it in your hearts to forgive my failings and weakness and you will do the same for others around you. In praying, Jesus himself said we should ask for forgiveness as we forgive those who hurt us. And I pray that you will continue to love me and remember I am as human as you are and will not always get things right.

CHAPTER THIRTY-NINE

Australia continues to be the country of my healing. A country that I had never dreamt of coming to, but God had other plans for me. I have cried many tears and yet had the best and longest laughs too. God has used complete strangers to speak in my life and in turn is encouraging me to reach out to help others heal.

My struggle with porn ended a few years ago through many prayers and a lot of stumbles. But God is a God of second chances and when we fall he always picks us up, dusts us off, and encourages us to keep pursuing him. Thankfully, he does not count how many times we fall, but looks forward to each time we get up and keep fighting. I am free and no longer a slave to anyone or to anything. God has indeed set me free. God has turned my shame into honour and fully embraced me and made me feel accepted not by man but himself. He continually shows me that I matter and should not look for approval, acceptance and definition from man but from him.

I have forgiven my family and friends who have hurt me. I go through seasons and something new happens that would trigger the past, and then the cycle of pain would start again. In those moments, I pray that God would give me his forgiveness so I could forgive them and others as Corrie Ten Boom prayed many years ago. He is faithful, and that's what he has done and continues to do in my life. My heart is free, the cycle has stopped, and my heart is full of joy and peace. I can bless those who hurt me, and I pray for each of them to find God and live a blessed life—John included. I would not wish God's wrath even on John. Everything else I leave to God. He will fight my battles. Just because God is slow to anger and slow to punish does not mean he is slack. He is full of grace and mercy and it is not his will that any will perish in their sin and darkness.

I have come to realise that if that visa had not come when it did I was literally going to lose my mind. I was breaking down, drowning and looking around I could not see anyone who cared enough to help me. I could not see a way out. I had held on for so long that I could not do it anymore. God showed up on time! God, Zane, and Australia became my go to in those dark years of my life. I am healed! I can think and talk about my life without breaking down for days and weeks on end. The panic attacks are far between and are becoming rarer. I have stopped condemning myself and thinking so low of myself to the point of defiling and punishing myself. I have also learned to forgive myself and my own shortcomings. God has healed my mind, my heart, my body, and for the first time in my life I feel whole!

I have learned very important lessons in my life. One is that *'All things work together for my good'* (Romans 8:28, GNB). Even those dark, painful moments I had have worked for my good. God did not kill my mother, sickness did. He allowed it to happen in his wisdom. And he has given me a peace so deep and quiet within me that I know I will see my mum and grandparents again and has confirmed this over and over again to me over the years. I am looking forward to an eternity with them.

He did not make my biological dad abandon me, that's a choice my dad made. He did not make John assault me, my stepmother and brothers hate me, nor did he make my dad behave and say the things he said. Those were choices made by free-willed human beings. But through it all, God himself has looked after me as a father would when a child falls and hurts himself. Through it all he has comforted me, taught me who he is and, most of all, gave me an inner peace that surpasses all understanding. He says to 'trust him with all my heart and lean not on my own understanding, and in all my ways I should acknowledge him and he will direct my path' (Proverbs 3:5, NIV). He surely does, as he promises, even though it is never in our time. He is never late nor early; he is always on time. His ways are not mine and neither are his thoughts my thoughts. He is also not human that he should lie and has put his word far above his name so what he says he will do, he does. And through it all, he is using my story to give hope to many others who seek his face and his council every day and those going through similar situations.

Looking back in my life, I realised just how strong God created me to be. He says he cannot give us more than we can bear (1 Corinthians 10:13, NIV), and I realise that I cannot walk another's journey, as I would not be able to endure their trials. We are all given our different strengths and endurance to be able to get through our own lives. Without him, I am nothing. But with him I have life and life everlasting. Faith, to me, is not something I do just on Sunday to tick a 'to-do' box, it is my life because I have tasted and seen the goodness of the Lord. I have also learnt there is always a way out, and it might seem slow in coming, but he always gives us a way out of every temptation.

A very important lesson I learned is that he is not only a father to the fatherless, but he brings people in this journey called life who take up the role of a parent to help you along the way. I have had so many mothers, fathers, and grandparent along the way who have enriched my life and helped me grow into the person I am today. I can truly say I was brought up by a village and the world. My girls, I pray that you will find people along your journey of faith and life who will bless you in this way too and help you grow into faithful godly women.

Perhaps the biggest comfort to me is that God says to me and to all of us to 'come as you are.' That's one of my favourite hymns too. God accepts my sin, darkened heart, sadness, pain, anger, bitterness, hopelessness, hate, and doubt. He just asks me to come to him as I am, and he cleans me up and slowly makes me like he is into his likeness. He is making me into purity, my rightful name. We all have dark secrets, dark sins that we think no other person knows about, or what we think are little sins, but where can one go to hide from God? Ignoring or denying his existence doesn't change the fact that he sees and knows our hearts.

Every religion in the world tries to reach God by asking the faithful to cleanse themselves, to offer sacrifices, have a list of dos and don'ts. Religion tries to build a bridge to God; it is man's effort to reach God but not a relationship with Christ. He knows we cannot make ourselves worthy of him. We cannot reach his standard. He doesn't demand perfection from us and that's a great comfort to me. He created the bridge between heaven and us. It is God's effort to rescue man. He did it all. He has paid the full price and all we have to do is to come to him wholeheartedly to receive the free gift of eternal life. He teaches us, he changes us, he corrects us, and he guides us, not from the outside but from the inside. Come just as you are and let him make you into the person he created you to be. I am glad I did, and though it has taken a while to get to where I am, I am still a work in progress and will be until the day I meet the Lord. And I am okay with that.

I thank God for Zane too who has seen me at my worst, and yet prayed for me and loved me anyway. He is full of love and patience and he is truly one of a kind, as Levi told me he would be many years ago. The name Zane means 'gift of God'. He is indeed a timely gift from God for me and he is a gift I really needed. Once again, God proved to me he does not sleep nor slumber, and that he is working in my life even when I can't see what he is doing. Zane is one of the biggest evidence of God's work. In this gift I found rest and peace.

I thank God for Australia, for indeed it is the land of my healing. I cry less now, I genuinely smile and laugh, I am no longer trying to prove myself to anyone and I no longer feel I'm not good enough (most of the time anyway). And once God is done with mending my fractured heart, he might just send us back to my homeland to keep doing his work there. In the meantime, while that door is still closed, I will bloom right here where I am planted and continue to serve those around me and those God brings along my way.

We live in one of Australia's lowest socio-economic suburbs. It is not because we cannot afford somewhere better or bigger but it is because there are people here hurting as I did. I see them every day, wanting a father or a mother, to be accepted, to belong. People who live here are constantly brushed aside and shunned by the very fact they live here. We have had a lot of people asking us why we would move into this neighbourhood and risk raising a family here. This question, surprisingly, is mostly asked by Christians. It is because I see myself in these people, and Zane and I would love to offer them hope and love and the acceptance they so crave. Our neighbours who have been through much and have so much more ahead in their lives, may seem to offer nothing to the world, but to us they offer perspective and keep us focused on what is more important in this life. That's the reason why our door is always open to all, so we can offer comfort and let them know they are not alone. I hope that through this, others will learn to be thankful for the blessings they have in their lives no matter how small and insignificant they seem. To whom much is given, much is expected. God has blessed me with much even if the world around me doesn't see it by the its standards and expectations. I will share the blessings with others.

God bless you my dear daughters. Take heart and be encouraged in Christ, pick up your crosses, and follow Christ. May this be an encouragement to you in your own faith walk with God.

Love, your mother and sister in Christ,
Purity.

EPILOGUE

I read an article in late 2015 about the child prostitutes on the Kenyan coast

(http://www.abc.net.au/7.30/content/2015/s4201189.htm,
http://gvnet.com/childprostitution/Kenya.htm,
https://www.youtube.com/watch?v=cdkhIW3QuVg).

These children are sometimes as young as six and come from all manner of backgrounds. Some have been trafficked there from different parts of the country and even from other countries, while others are locals being encouraged by relatives to be prostitutes. This is because there's a belief that the quickest way to get out of poverty is by getting an older white man. There are a lot of willing customers, white older men, who are mostly in their sixties and even as old as eighties. These men come to the coast for holidays and pay to have this underage girl experience. Other sources report the number of child prostitutes to be about 40,000. It saddens my heart to hear that this industry is thriving.

A few years ago I visited Zanzibar and learnt of another heartbreaking arrangement. There are lots of older European men who keep local wives—often much younger African girls. They spend six months in Europe with their legal wives and then come to Africa for the next six months. This, I was informed, happens all along the East African coast.

These two situations fill me with anger and sadness. I know how it feels to be used for things. How demoralizing it is but it has been made to look like it is okay. Instead of the industry ebbing into nothingness, it is growing even bigger. How I pray that it will end, that tourists and locals will treat each other as human beings, that the tourists will take a moment to imagine their daughters experiencing what they are subjecting these children / young women to, that the locals will realise the damage they are causing the girls by selling them to prostitution.

I have heard of a lot of stories of girls who have gone through what I have and they ended up being prostitutes, as I wanted to. There's still hope for you. You can turn your life around. You can be set free and you can be healed. I hope and pray that my story will encourage you and show you there is a way out. There is one who can bring light into the darkness and will set you free. His name is Jesus.

INDEX

Printed in the United States
By Bookmasters